Name Me Nobody

Name Me Nobody

Lois-Ann Yamanaka

HYPERION PAPERBACKS
NEW YORK

First Hyperion Paperback Edition 2000
1 3 5 7 9 10 8 6 4 2
Printed in the United States of America.
This book is set in Waldbaum Book.
Library of Congress Cataloging-in-Publication Data
Yamanaka, Lois-Ann, 1961–
Name me nobody/Lois-Ann Yamanaka.—1st ed.
p. cm.
Summary: Emi-Lou struggles to come of age
in her middle-school years in Hawaii.
ISBN 0-7868-0452-1 (trade).—ISBN 0-7868-2394-1 (lib.)
ISBN 0-7868-1466-7 (pbk.)
[1. Schools—Fiction. 2. Hawaii—Fiction.] I. Title.
PZ7.Y19155Nam 1999
[Fic]—dc21 98-43251
Visit www.hyperionteens.com

For Shari Nakamura, Nancy Hoshida, Claire Shimizu, Donna Hamane, Don Sumada, and Melvin Everett Spencer III, golden kine

For Pono Kunishima, Marisa Sue Pang, Marci Kiyoko Tagawa, Angela and Rex Matsuo, Lian and Leiah Fournier, Alisha Macapagal, and Jordan M. Harrison, the Friday Night Writing Club

Contents

Name Me Nobody

1.
Name Me

I have a feeling that my obsession with names started with my mother, Roxanne Kaya. They all called her Rocky because she was stubborn like a rock. But the truth be known, all the boys loved my mother. She was gorgeous and got everything she wanted. She got everything, all right. And then she had me. My mother was sixteen when I was born.

She briefly considered naming me Carly, for Carly Simon. I'd have been Carly Kaya, named for the "You're So Vain" album. But the name reminded my mother of Carly Espinoza, a softball pitcher for the Pāhoa Angels. She didn't pluck in between her eyebrows so they used to call her Mono-brow. Bad luck, my mother thought. I might turn out facially hairy.

As the story goes, my mother, on a pop singer roll, then thought to name me Linda for Linda Rondstadt. But there was a two-hundred-pounder chick from Kapoho whose name was Linda. Bad luck again. I might turn out fat, but that happened anyway.

So I was named Emi-lou for Emmylou Harris. My mother used to do it to the *Profile* album. So they say. The words to those songs made her cry. After I was born, she listened to Emmylou Harris and cried every day for a month.

But good fortune came to my mother with the name Emi-lou: I never cry.

Emi-lou with a Japanese spelling, Emi-lou for the nights of the folk singer playing over and over on some boy's eight-track car stereo.

They say my mother was confused. She *became* Catholic when she got pregnant—all of a sudden against abortion, Rocky and the Pope himself. She wanted to irk my grandma. She wanted to draw attention to her big belly. She wanted to bring the baby to the May Day pageant like all the other girls. It was the in thing to do for the teenage mommy, daddy, and newborn baby.

And my father? That's one name they never mention. They say that the word *bastard* doesn't apply to girls. It only refers to boys who don't have fathers. But that's what I am. A nobody bastard girl.

2.
War Names

My grandma says, "Okay, Roxanne, the girl don't need a name. She has a good one. She's a Kaya. But give her some clarity and tell her who her daddy is. Who the hell is Emi-lou's father? You no think she deserves to know?"

My grandma said this after our New Year's party last year. My mother had flown home to Hilo from beauty school, but she stayed with some boyfriend in Pāhoa. I hardly saw her at all. My mother keeps this secret to irk my grandma's mind.

My grandma tells me on New Year's Day, "No worry, Emi-lou. I tell you one secret. My real name not Leatrice." She serves me ozoni soup with a big mochi melting in the broth. We drink this soup every New Year's Day for good luck, Grandma and I. We've celebrated by ourselves for years.

"World War Two time, I had to change my name." The steam from the soup fogs up her glasses. "I use to be Reiko. That's my middle name, right?"

Grandma makes a small serving in a nice chawan for Grandpa even though he's been dead a long time now. She puts his bowl on the table. "But you know what? Not having my real name no hurt me at all."

I know what Grandma's trying to say.

"One day, I came home from school with a letter from my elementary school teacher. It said we Japs have to prove that we good, loyal Americans. We have to change our Japanese names. You believe that? After I read that to my mother, she said, 'Okay. What name you like?'"

My grandma drinks deeply from her bowl. "I was stunned," she goes on. "'What name you like, Reiko-chan?' my mother ask me again."

"What you said to her, Grandma?" I ask her.

"'Nothing,'" she says and then she pauses. "'Name me nobody.'"

"'Bakatare!' my mother yell at me," she says.

"You ain't stupid, Grandma. You the smartest person I know."

My grandma nods. "Finally, I said Leatrice," she says. "My favorite teacher used to be Miss Leatrice Cherry. I thought her name match her. Leatrice Cherry and she had red hair. But I never have red hair. My mother wrote down L-e-a-t-r-i-c-e. Was too late. Now that I think about it, I wish I name myself Ellen. That's nicer, what you think?"

I bite into a circle of translucent daikon. "You have a good name, Grandma," I tell her.

She looks away from me. "My sister Hatsuko, she name herself Nancy for Nancy Drew, I guess," my grandma says. "Teruko became Janis from the Bible. My brother, Hikaru, name himself Ken, like Barbie husband. And my older brother, Torao, became Harry. The swinger, I call him. But all of us, we never mind, you know, Emi-lou. We just went on like any other day."

I have to hear that every time the newly named Roxanne Kaye leaves for California again. Names don't matter because we're all really family under the skin.

As far as I gather from my years of eavesdropping on adult conversations, I was conceived during Bon Dance season when the Japanese call the dead back to earth. I was born the following March. My mother still had time to go to the junior prom.

They say that two guys came around at that time. One was Jerry Rapoza, the lifeguard at the Pāhoa pool. He wasn't even in school. He had graduated long before, but Roxanne was messing around with him.

My mother was also seeing Kenneth Miranda. He was a year older than her. I found letters and newspaper clippings in my mother's yearbook. Kenneth played baseball. He was an all-island, first-team pick for the *Hilo Tribune Herald*.

But like I said, I don't care. After my mother ditched me when I was three, and my grandma was forced to adopt me, Roxanne first renamed herself Goldie, for Goldie Hawn in *Butterflies Are Free*. She went platinum blonde, painted a wildflower on her face, and left for San Francisco as Goldie Kaye.

My own mother, she never talks to me, never calls me, doesn't send me anything for my birthday like she never gave birth to me. That's why, I always say to myself, if she doesn't care, then I don't care.

My grandpa used to tell me, "Stop nagging. You cannot see your mommy. She no live by Disneyland."

I thought California *was* Disneyland.

"No Disneyland for you. You too naughty."

For a long time, I thought maybe that's why only Roxanne got to go. I was so naughty that she was forced to leave me behind.

3.

School Names

The popular Japanese girls name me on a daily basis.

"Hey, Emi-lump, I want a bite of your doughnut." I was eating my breakfast outside of my homeroom.

They always purse their shiny lips at me. "Emi-oink," they say as they lift their noses with their index fingers. Their subclique of wanna-bes giggle like a Greek chorus.

I'm not smart enough to be a nerd. I'm not stink enough to be a turd. I fall somewhere right below the band geeks and right above the zeroes.

"Emi-fat, eat a rat, tell your mother you get major cellulite." It's a lousy rhyme, but why bother pointing it out over all of the laughter? This is the clever singsong of a so-called friend, social ladder climber, almost a wanna-be but still a student gov geek, Judith Wong.

I hate the intermediate school, which haoles on TV call middle school. We have elementary school and they have grammar school. Whatever, just names.

Sometimes the Jap-girls call me Emi-loser. Sometimes they call me Emi-lez. And this they say behind my back because my best friend in this cruddy school is Yvonne Vierra.

Yvonne calls herself Von. And so what if Von loves me? I don't care who knows or what they say. I do have feelings for her, but not the way the high and almighty popular ones think.

About the same time she names herself Von, she nicknames me Louie. "No more of those other stupid names. Jap punks," she mutters. "Treating you bad when I not around. They just wait."

She always hangs out in the bathroom with the rugged titas during first recess and lunch recess. I'm way too geeky for the rugged and Von's way too cool for any hangout but the shop bathroom, so I stick around Rudy Rudman.

The popular Jap-girls never tease me when they see me with Von. I like the name Louie. It makes me tough like Von for a moment. "But Louie sounds like Lumpy," I tell her.

"No it don't. I slap them silly if they even try it," she says. "I cannot wait till they open their big mouths in front of me, Louie. Me and you, from now on, we Von and Louie." She takes a black Sharpie out of her pocket and writes V-a-L on the bench outside of the bathroom at JCPenney. "So they don't ever forget it." Von shoves her pen in her pocket, then pats my back. "Kaya's a good last name. I like it."

"But it's my grandma's name," I tell her.

"So? At least it's a name." Von never tires of this conversation. That's why I love her.

"I feel shame, that's all," I tell her. "I mean, a mother and a father, that's normal. And the kid suppose to have the father's last name. And the mother and father go to piano recital and band concerts to watch the kid perform."

"Your grandma goes. Your grandma's name is good," Von repeats as she tries to console me. "Even if your mother changed her last name from Kaya to Kaye, never mind."

"Never mind that she haolified herself?"

"Never mind," Von says with a crooked smile.

"I know why I don't have a real last name," I tell her. "I don't have a father."

"Scientifically impossible," Von says.

"Not if he's a secret."

In the absence of a mother and father, I've made a family for myself. Von became my protector, my sister. When I was a little girl my grandma often said, "Emilou, you move around the world afraid of your own shadow, unless you with Yvonne."

In Ivy Nursery School, Von held my hand throughout the day and protected me from the girl bullies who were quick with their hands and words. Von was quicker for the both of us, so quick she nearly got expelled from preschool. At lunch, she sat beside me and opened my Tupperware containers full of grapes or Ritz crackers. She covered me with her blanket at nap time.

When we were six, Von used her father's sickle to forge a trail for me through the thick honohono grass to get to the grove of wood roses and wild orchids that I picked for her. I arranged them in a vase with red anthuriums and pink gladiolas stolen from my neighbor's yard, stolen for Von.

When we were nine, Von convinced me that we'd be real sisters if the blood in our veins was the same. She took a sewing needle from my grandma's pincushion and hid with me under the house. I pressed the joint at the tip of my index finger until it throbbed red-white.

"Us against the world," Von said as she broke the skin on my finger, easing the blood out. She took the needle and poked the tip of her finger. Then she pressed her finger to mine, twisting and winding our fingertips together. "We will always be together."

4.
Lez

"**W**hat you mean the two of us together, Uncle Charlie? Me, too? I playing for the Hilo Astros? They want me to play for them?"

Of course, I cannot believe that they would want me. I mean, I'm not terribly unathletic, just kind of fat and slow. I'm definitely not the last girl the teams pick in P.E. That plug of a life-form is Bambi Mori, the least popular girl with zits upon zits and a colony of plaque growing on her braces.

"Yeah, you," Uncle tells me and picks his teeth with his baby fingernail. "I already told the coach. Where Yvonne go, Emi-lou go. Like it or lump it. She never call my bluff. She said, 'Okay then, Charlie, whatever you say.'"

"That's because they want Von bad. She the baddest third baseman in this whole district," I tell him. Von feels good about herself. I can tell.

"Stop calling her Von, Emi-lou. And you, Yvonne, no call her Louie, you hear me? They all might think you're a couple of . . . of . . . sheez, just listen to me–"

Aunty Etsuko stops washing the dishes. "Charlie, my dear," she says, "come help me, okay? Don't mind him, girls. He's just being tense, as usual."

They don't want to say the words *lesbian* or *butchie*. But it's all around us in this town, at the high schools and intermediate schools, ball games, the mall, the beach, cruising Banyan Drive, the game rooms, pool halls, concerts, movies—tough aunties with pretty girl-friends, uncles with soft voices and buffed bodies, and uncles who are sometimes aunties all mingling and hanging out at our parties and family gatherings.

I look at Von and then at Uncle Charlie. He's wrong. I know her inside, outside, all the way around and back. She just can't be. No way. She's not like that because I'm not like that. V-a-L, right?

"Well, you know what that women's softball league is like, rights, Ets?" Uncle Charlie says. "Been like that since we was kids. Those wahines all so . . . man, they all so short hair, man clothes, truck driving . . . so damn ballsy—"

"Stereo—" Von begins.

"Typing," her mother finishes.

"Not," Uncle grumbles, "I not stereo-whatevers."

"I like coming to your house, *Yvonne*," I tell her. "I learn a lot of new words, *Yvonne*." Everybody laughs except for Uncle Charlie.

On the Big Island, we don't have a bobby-sox league, just a big women's softball league. There's teams from Kona, Kohala, Puna, Ka'u and Hāmākua. No age restriction. That's why Von could play, even if she was only fourteen.

The best girls get recruited in the ninth grade. Lots of Hilo girls get scholarships to play collegiate softball. It's their ticket out. Softball evens the playing field with the rich Japanese, Chinese, and haoles.

"What you think, Louie?" Von asks me. "Which team should I pick? Help me pick."

"I don't know," I tell Von. "You like me ask my aunty Vicky? I ask her after school today when she come home from work." Aunty Vicky's ten years older than us. She's been playing for the Hilo Astros since the ninth grade.

"Vicky going to tell me play for the Hilo Astros," Von says. "I know she your aunty, but tell the truth, Louie—she no irk your mind? Always calling you Fat Albert and Big Hunk, pushing you around . . . "

"She only mean to her family. She nice to her friends," I tell Von. "So she gotta have some niceness inside her, what you think?"

"I doubt it," Von mutters. "She nasty, Louie."

"She use to be the baby of the family—till I came along to 'ruin things' as she always says."

"Cuts no ice with me," Von says. "She just one big baby who gotta grow up and get used to it."

"You play for the Hilo Astros," Uncle Charlie breaks in. "They the best team in the Big Island Women's Softball League 'cause plenty of their girls went Hilo College on four-year scholarship. Some even went to UH-Mānoa. The coaches get connections. And they not . . . not all . . . butchies. Okay, Ets, there—I said it."

"Von ain't," I whisper. "Me, too. I ain't. We not, Uncle Charlie, promise."

He's watching for a reaction from Von. But she just looks away and smiles.

"So what, Louie-Louie," she says, "you like one more pork chop?"

"Fattening," I tell her. "Half-half, me and you."

Uncle Charlie gets mad when we skirt the subject with our flippant remarks about pork chops. "You like me slap you silly?" he asks. "I make you two titas walk to softball practice for the first couple of weeks, you wait." He stabs the pork chop and slaps it onto my plate. "Start your diet tomorrow."

"Vicky was chubby just like Emi-lou, right, Charlie?" Aunty Etsuko says as she sits down at the table. "Your aunty lost a lot of weight playing ball. And you have such a cute face. Imagine if you lost a few pounds. You'd be the spitting image of your mother. And look at Vicky. She's so slender now."

"She still has a big fat mouth," Von says.

Von's right. Even if Aunty Vicky's skinny, she still has her grouchy, fatheaded personality. I've heard this lose weight lecture so many times before. And to me, the word *chubby* always negates the whole cute face comment.

"Even if you don't get to play," Aunty Ets continues, "it'll be good for you to get out there and run around. And you can keep Yvonne company."

"It could be in your genes," Von whispers to me. I'd told her about one of my father possibilities, Kenneth Miranda, who went on to play baseball at a junior college on the mainland.

"Maybe," I tell her. "I just hate sweating. I not totally junk, right, Von? You seen me play in P.E."

"You okay," she says. "You kick my ass in Ping-Pong."

"I pretty good at racquet sports. How come I so junk in other sports?"

"You choke, Louie," Von tells me as she slathers her pork chop in ketchup and A-1. "You all right when you only worrying about yourself, but you always choke when you play team sports."

"Too much pressure," I tell her. "I hate that. When you make mistake, they all blaming you for losing the game. You gotta worry too much about everybody else."

"Just relax. I be there to back you up," Von reassures me. "You for choke, I tell you."

"That's why when me and Vicky challenge you two scrubs in doubles, we wipe you off the court," Uncle Charlie brags.

Von gives him a dirty look. "I seen worse," she says. "We be starting together, Louie. You hit pretty good."

"Big deal. You get more experience. They let you play with the boys in the pony league. And they kept promoting you."

"Until I grew tits." Von laughs, punching my arm. "See, Louie, now you can play because it's a women's league. V-a-L, right? No more sitting in the stands. Do it for me, please."

"You really like me play, Von?"

"For me, Louie, play. I mean, they all older than me. Otherwise, I the only freshman kid coming in."

I can do this for Von. I know it's her ticket out. Softball might be the only way she can get a college scholarship. Maybe she'll feel comfortable after a while and I can be the bat girl. Maybe I can lose a few pounds in the process. "I starting my diet tomorrow," I tell her. Von smiles as she serves herself more rice. "I doing this for you."

5.

One Big, Happy Ohana

Uncle Charlie drives us up to Carvalho Park for our first practice with the Hilo Astros. The baseball field, covered in a light drizzle, looks varnished in white. "No be scared, okay, Louie?" Von tells me. She knows I can't handle myself too well around rugged people, but Von fits right in. "Just let me do all the talking, okay, Louie? You choking already?"

I nod my head and Uncle Charlie says, "No tell Emilou what to do, Yvonne. Sometimes, you just like your mother. So bossy." We walk past the wet aluminum bleachers. "There her. Erma Kaaina, your coach."

"Eh, Charlie, my main man," she says, kicking mud off her cleats. "Let me see—which one of these two is your daughter? Has to be this one, the one who look Portagee like you. You lucky that stuck-up Japanee girl married you, you ugly Portagee, you. What her name? Suka? Etsuki? Her name no matter—at least now, your girl half-smart."

"She *is* smart," I mutter.

Von says nothing. She's always thinking she's half-stupid from her Portuguese father's side. The Portuguese jokes here are like the Polish jokes I heard a comedian telling on TV. Von always thinks she's the punchline.

"What?" Coach Kaaina says.

"Nothing," Von answers.

"She not stupid," I whisper. Von nudges me hard.

Von's in the medium English and the low social studies classes. I don't know why. She isn't dumb to me. The teachers think we don't know about high, medium, or low sections. But we do. It makes some kids feel like turds, that is, those of us turds not labeled gifted and talented.

Von's in the gifted and talented math class with all the smart and popular Jap-girls. She figures the teachers misplaced her, but she gets all *B*'s. That's pretty smart to me.

"No need get all hu-hu," Coach Kaaina says. "Yvonne, pretty soon you be one of *my girls*. Take a joke, okay, kid?" She whispers to Uncle, "Touchy, just like the mother, eh, Charlie?" Then jerking her chin to me, she asks, "And who's this?"

"I told you about this one–our family friend. We been like family even before these two kids were born. This is Emi-lou Kaya. You know her grandmother, Leatrice? The retired schoolteacher," Uncle Charlie says. "She play A-flight with you in the Hilo Women's Golf Club. Leatrice, the nine-handicapper."

"Oh?" Coach Kaaina says, nodding slowly and looking me over. "You Leatrice's granddaughter? Who your mother, Roxanne or Amy?"

Von speaks up for me. "Roxanne, but she working on the mainland, so her grandma take care of her."

"Ooohhh?" Coach Kaaina says kind of sassily. She's surprised by Von's defensive tone. There's a long pause. "Well, come meet all the girls." She walks us onto the muddy field. The girls throw the ball around, snapping in wet gloves to warm up.

"Maybe you lose some of your baby fat," Coach Kaaina tells me. "Just like your aunty Vicky. She had some thunder thighs when she first joined the team. About your age." My aunty Vicky jogs over to us. She takes off her glove and tucks it under her arm.

"Eh, Von," she says.

"Whassup? What about Louie?" Von says to Aunty Vicky. "Say hi to your niece."

"Eh, Chubs," she says, hitting the back of my head with her glove. "Pretty hefty shadow you get, Von."

"Ha ha, very funny," I tell her.

"Wise up, Emi-lou," Aunty Vicky says.

"Never lip-off to my older girls," Coach Kaaina says as she lights a long brown cigarette, "you punk brownies hear me?" She glares at me and I lower my eyes.

"This is Rae Kalani," she tells us as she points toward a tall woman with short, curly hair, "the best first baseman in the whole women's league." She flicks ash and exhales a thin line of smoke. "And this is one of the best pitchers in the nation, Choochie Ah Chong. What's your real name?" Coach Kaaina asks.

"Merla," the girl says in a voice that surprises me, it's so soft. "You making me shame, Aunty Erma."

"Chooch play for Hilo College, NAIA first team pick last season, and one of my girls in the off-season. And this here is my Babes," Coach Kaaina says, hugging the next girl tightly. "Kris Hinano, catcher. NCAA scouts from the mainland already looking at her."

Babes smiles at Von. I thought maybe they had met each other before and were trying to figure out how and where. Babes looks husky, but not full-on chubby like me. Maybe she has big muscles. Definitely no flab. And definitely an attitude.

Coach Kaaina sends her cigarette butt twirling away, then gently touches the braided hair of the next girl. "This pretty little thing is Viva Ching." I look at Von to give her the eye that this is the one who works for Uncle Charlie after school as a receptionist. "Sixteen, same age as Babes."

"No ask me for one raise now, Genevieve," Uncle Charlie says, "unless you good to Emi-lou and Yvonne. Then I think about it." He puts his huge arms around the two of us.

The rest of the girls sit in the dugout. Coach Kaaina says, "We got lots of time to meet everybody later. Make yourself at home. We just like one big, happy ohana, all my girls and me."

6.
Ain't No Quitter

Some big, happy ohana. Only *her* girls call her Aunty Erma.

Her girls make double plays. "That's my girl, Babes, hana hou!"

They pitch no-hitters. "Chooch, you my girl. Keep the arm healthy. Move down, Chubs. Let Chooch sit next to me."

They hit the right cut-off man. "Atta girl, Vicky. That's using your head."

They hit singles. "Good girl, Viva."

Doubles. "RBI, Rae-girl, bring in the RBIs."

Triples. "You go, Babes. You go, girlfriend."

Home runs. "That's my girl, Herline."

Her girls catch fly balls, steal bases, plow into home plate, and remember her signals.

Her girls bring her fresh kulolo and hot fish cake from Amano's. "You girls always thinking about your Aunty Erma." She smooches the ones bearing gifts before practice.

But like I said, I'm really doing this for Von. "No let them intimidate you," I tell her before she bats. "Base hit into right field and show um your wheels."

Before one of our practices, I hand Von a warm package. "Give these lemon bars to Coach Kaaina. Tell her *you* made them."

"But you did," Von says.

"Never mind, you need to give um to her, not me." The next day, I make Von give her my secret recipe ice cream cookies, then blond brownies that I make from scratch. I pull out all the stops with my hand-dipped chocolate strawberries. "You be one of her girls," I tell Von, "via her stomach."

"What about you?" Von asks.

"I eat the leftovers," I tell her. "How you think I keep my girlish figure?" Von ruffles my hair.

"You think of me twenty-four-seven," Von says with a small smile.

"Let me tape your fingers," I tell her as I take a roll of athletic tape from my backpack. "Coach Kaaina gotta put you in the lineup for sure if you keep upping your stats."

In turn, Von encourages me every day to never give up. "If you quit, she win," Von reminds me. "For me, Louie. Show me you ain't no quitter."

"Coach Kaaina hate me," I tell her.

"You too girly-girly. Try run and move with less frills–watch me."

"She absolutely hate me," I mutter.

"You too airhead. You gotta listen. You ain't uncoachable. C'mon, Louie."

"I do, I promise, I want to get better for you, Von."

"You cannot be doing the drills half-ass. You gotta sweat, Louie, no biggie. No pain, no strain, no gain."

"I ain't no quitter."

"Put your heart into the basic skills. Over and over is the only way you get better. Pay attention. I seen you picking flowers in right field. Show her what you made of."

"Flab."

"No choke, Louie. C'mon, relax. Let it flow."

Every day, Von gives me a mighty pep talk. Every day, I make sure Von is in prime mental condition to kick ass. And I will make sure that Coach Kaaina comes to know the Von that I know.

We practice basic skills and batting with Uncle Charlie early in the morning. "Louie," Von always says, "you have to believe in yourself."

"Cliché, cliché, cliché," I tell her. "I believe in music."

"So what if I talk cliché?" Von says. "Sports—no, life—is full of clichés. So you reach for the stars, put your heart and soul in everything you do, show her what you made of, never give up. What's wrong with all that?"

"Nothing," I mumble.

Von kneads my shoulders, palms my back hard, and pumps me up. Then she pushes me toward the field. I trip.

So I'm the worst player on the Hilo Astros roster. "Keep your head up," Coach Kaaina yells at me. "What you doing looking at your feet? Heads up, heads up. Be alert. You one waste of my damn time."

I'm not quick enough on my feet. She whips the ball

at my head on some days, or rolls the ball to me real slowly on other days and tells me, "Your legs ain't roots. Let's see you move those tree trunks. Move it. Take two laps. You too damn fat. Sheez."

I'm the fat bat girl. "C'mon grab those bats. I don't want any of my girls hurt because of a good-for-nothing slow ass daydreamer. Pay attention!"

I'm the water girl. "Make yourself useful. Bring a cooler of ice to practice," she snarls at me.

I'm the statistician at the end of the bench. "I thought Japs suppose to be good at stats? Be accurate or these numbers is useless to me."

I run even more laps if I miss *one* fly ball that Coach Kaaina hits way over my head on purpose. But I don't care.

My aunty Vicky's so ashamed of my lousy softball skills. She acts like we're not even family. I don't care. I'm doing this for Von, and she would do the same for me.

I'm playing on the Hilo Astros women's softball team because I know if I'm there at every practice, every game, every party, every out-of-town doubleheader, I can be with Von.

So no matter what Coach Kaaina says or does, I will not quit. It's not about her. I have to play. I will sit on the cold aluminum bleachers all day and all night if I have to. Uncle Charlie's suspicions quietly nag at me. I want her to stay normal. I want Von to come home with me.

7.
Hapa and Beautiful

The last weekend in June, the Hilo Astros, along with boyfriends, husbands, girlfriends, babies, cousins, sisters, brothers, you name it, plan a camping trip to Puakō. Coach Kaaina owns a beach house on the sweltering west coast of the Big Island.

Right before we leave, my grandma says, "Vicky, you better be responsible for these kids. Hanging around with all you troublemaking–"

"And Vicky, watch out for Yvonne, too," Uncle Charlie adds. "Maybe we better go down this Saturday and bring some ono okazu for the girls, what you think, Lea?"

"No, Daddy," Von whines. "We know you like check up on us. Nothing going to happen, right, Louie? 'Cause we don't do the stuff that some of the other girls do."

"You see what I mean?" my grandma says. "Like what kind other *stuff*? Vicky, you listen to me–you keep these two out of trouble."

"Yeah, yeah, yeah. Always about Louie since the day she was born," Aunty Vicky mutters. "I getting sick and tired of watching Louie. She not even mine."

"Don't you yeah, yeah, yeah me, Victoria Jean Kaya. I still supporting you. So wise up before you find yourself out the door. For good."

Uncle Charlie throws his poker hand down and grabs a handful of Planters cocktail nuts. "We be there on Saturday," he says. "Erma love Japanee food. Expect us."

"Ho, Daddy," Von groans as she lifts her backpack and her sleeping bag. "C'mon, Louie. We go wait outside. Babes picking us up in her new Comanche." We walk to the back door.

"Comanche?" Uncle Charlie yells. "No tell me you two knuckleheads riding in the back of a truck all the way down the Hāmākua coast? You see what I mean about these two kids, Lea. They think they smarter than us. You riding in the back of the girl's truck, Yvonne?"

"No, Daddy," Von grumbles. "We all squeezing in the front. If too crowded, we can jump in Coach Kaaina's van when we stop at Kamuela Deli. No worry. Sheez."

Babes comes screeching up the driveway. Von and I throw our sleeping bags and backpacks into the bed of the truck. Babes opens the door from the inside and says, "Hurry up, get in. I picking up my cousin and his friend down Pana'ewa."

Von gets in first and I sit by the window. The night air rushes in my face. Babes drives like she's acting big. Speeding and cutting the corners, she burns out at the light by the KTA Store. She lights a cigarette, her arm hanging out of the window like a fat cop.

She pulls into a long gravel driveway. When we get to the garage, two figures emerge from the dark and into the headlights. "Ho, cuz, howzit," Babes says. "Jump in, you guys."

"That's Kyle Kiyabu?" Von asks. "He your cousin, Babes? He played middle blocker for Hilo High from his freshman year?"

"Yup," Babes says. "His father and my mother are brother and sister. His father married one haole. My mother married one Hawaiian. So we both hapa and beautiful, I guess."

"Eh, whassup?" Kyle says as he high-fives his cousin. "Babes, this my friend Sterling, Aunty Erma's grandson from Pāhoa. We jumping in her van in Kamuela, 'cause we refuse to freeze our balls back here." The boys high-five and shake hands macho-style.

Kyle leans his head on the glass right against my head, and omigod, I feel his heat. He's the handsomest thing I ever saw in the last two Hilo High yearbooks. He was a dreamboat for the Keywanettes Club, a homecoming escort his freshman and sophomore year, and a prince representing the Big Island in the last two May Day pageants.

I'm so concerned about Kyle Kiyabu that I tune out Von and Babes's conversation. I'm too busy looking at Kyle in the side mirror. I try to look bad with my arm hanging out of the window even if I'm freezing cold.

Babes moves her arm on the seat-back behind Von. I glance at Babes. Short hair, man clothes, drives a truck, ballsy—and now, she's acting like Von's boyfriend. So I think fast. "Babes, I can have one cigarette?" I ask.

"You no even smoke," Von says. "Why you trying for act hot? Stupid." Von never calls me stupid.

"No call me stupid. I *do* smoke," I tell her.

"No need act tough," Babes says. "Just us. Relax."

"Since when you smoke?" Von asks. "Since Kyle sitting back there? You choking, Louie," Von tells me from between gritted teeth.

"So where the cigs?" I ask. Von chuckles as Babes gets a cigarette from her bag. I put my arm on the seatback behind Von.

"Bust a gut," she says as she passes it to me. I stare her straight in the eye. I don't want her sitting so close to Von. I don't want her to get too friendly.

By the time we get to Kamuela, it's so cold that Kyle and Sterling have opened our sleeping bags to keep warm. Kyle says, "We go down Puakō in the truck, what you think, Sterling? Whose sleeping bag I was using?"

Omigod, Kyle Kiyabu in *my* sleeping bag. "That's Emi-lou's. We call her Louie."

"Whose? Yours?" Kyle makes a funny face like I don't rate to have him use my sleeping bag to keep warm. But I don't care. That's Kyle Kiyabu in my sleeping bag and I'll never wash it again.

"Here, give um to me," Sterling says. "I use um. I can?"

"He talking to you," Von says, giving me a nudge. "Answer."

I nod quickly. "Whatever," I tell him trying to act cool.

"Whatever?" Von laughs. "Choke," she whispers.

Kyle holds my sleeping bag with two fingers like it's

full of contagious fatso germs. Sterling takes it and wraps it around himself. "Thanks, Amy Lou."

"Louie," Von corrects him. "Emi, not Amy."

"Okay, whatever, sorry." He smiles. "Tally-ho, Babes," Sterling says as we all get back in the truck and take the winding road down to the beach house at Puakō.

The sea air smells briny at night, the sweet damp aroma of kiawe trees lingering along the beachfront road. Cars, trucks, and vans line the driveway to Coach Kaaina's house. Rubber slippers splay in random order by the front door. Everyone's sleeping on the living room floor and out on the lanai.

Babes puts her sleeping bag down. I unroll mine quickly and grab my pillow. I throw my sleeping bag and pillow next to Babes's sleeping bag and pillow. I can't take any chances on short hair, man clothes, truck-driving, ballsy stereotyping. I can't seem to get Uncle Charlie's words out of my head.

I pat the empty space beside me for Von. She unrolls her bedding slowly, like she knows what I'm up to, keeping her away from Babes and close to me. She doesn't say a word.

Good.

I say, "Good night, Von. Let's go to Hāpuna early in the morning, okay? Maybe your father no can find us. What you think?"

Von says, "Yeah, whatevers, Louie." She elbows me hard.

Nobody, not even Babes, can come between us. The looks they give each other, the way they move and touch each other when they talk, I don't like it.

8.
White Whale

Coach Kaaina boils lots of eggs and pan-fries Portuguese sweet bread for breakfast. A bunch of us grab some food and juice and pile in Babes's truck with our towels, bags, sand boards, and boogie boards.

The water at Hāpuna Beach is blue like a river in heaven. Everybody spreads their goza and towels and Von runs to the water. "C'mon, Louie," she yells back at me.

I sit uncomfortably on my mat. Usually I charge into the water with Von. Uncle Charlie and Grandma have to scream and yell before we come back to the shady pavillion near the showers. But here in front of all the girls and especially Kyle, I feel ashamed of my fat.

"C'mon. We go swim," Sterling says to me, motioning toward the water.

I whisper a soft, "No, thanks."

"Leave your tank top on," he whispers back. "Look all the titas out there with tank top and bikini bottom. No shame."

"Nah, I no like," I tell him, "maybe later." I try to back away from him.

"Then just come with us by the water. Just wet your feet," he insists.

Von runs back to get me. "Hurry up, Louie. We can sand board. It's low tide. Eh, what's with you, man?" I pull off my shorts slowly. "She better than me at sand boarding," she brags to Sterling.

"Ho, put your shorts back on," Kyle yells. "We getting blinded by the sight of white whale blubber, no, Sterling? Ho, thar she blow."

My aunty Vicky's right there. She's the one who laughs the loudest. "Hey, hey, hey," she says, "it's Fat Albert."

"No, Moby Dick," Kyle adds.

"Eh, what you said?" Von comes right up to Kyle. "I no care if you Babes's cousin. When you hang with the girls, no be cutting us down."

"Yeah, like she one of you girls. She never played one minute in one game. All I seen her do is pick up bats," Kyle says, "and even that, she ain't too good."

Sterling passes a towel to me and I quickly wrap it around my waist. He gets between Kyle and Von and nudges her away from him with his body.

"Her *name* is Louie," Von says. Babes comes over and stands next to Kyle. "Chill, cuz."

"Yeah, yeah, yeah. C'mon, Sterling," Kyle yells as he heads toward the water. He laughs as he runs off doing a baby elephant walk.

Sterling shrugs his shoulders and shakes his head. He turns to look at me and tries to say something, but Von signals him to go away.

I feel so humiliated. My thighs feel like two tons of flabby butter melting into the sand. Von sits next to me. "Louie," she says softly, "the hell with him. Pass me my bag. I bought this QT at Hilo Drugs special for you. Supposed to make you tan fast. You all white 'cause we been playing too much softball. No time to go beach anymore, yeah?" She bumps me gently with her shoulder.

"Stop trying to make me feel better. You always do that."

"Why? You do the same for me, more even." I look at Von. She's naturally tanned. I'm white like a haole. Von rubs the QT on my back and says, "We just sit here and catch some rays first. He's a punk, Louie. And I know you think he cute—no need say nothing right this minute—but Louie, he ain't nothing, man."

"He just kidding around," I tell her, choking back my shame. "I can take a joke." I put my head down and Von punches my arm.

"And that other thing he said. Louie, you ever want a boyfriend, then, girlfriend, you better lose some pounds," Von says. "You on the Von-plan until school start."

"Yeah, right," I tell her, "I tried everything."

"But you did it by yourself. I ain't smart, but you know I only half-dumb. Put our two heads together, we figure something out. I be your trainer. We swim some laps, sand board, body surf—I tell you, Louie, by the time I pau with you, Kyle going regret what he said today."

"Right," I tell her.

Von runs toward the water. She turns and hold up

her index finger. "You got me in you, remember?" she yells. Von runs up behind Babes Hinano and throws her into the surf. Their limbs tangle as they laugh, splashing water at each other, and dunking each other's heads in the waves.

The sun is surrounded with yellow and white rings above us. I watch as Von sand boards across the tide, cutting the surface, hitting the lip of the wave and gliding back to me. The sky is a natural blue. And Von glistens in the rising tide.

9.
Von's Femme

The QT made my skin orange.

I look tanned up until the time I come home. I walk past the hallway mirror. I'm the color of an orangutan.

Aunty Vicky's in the living room. I can see and hear her from the bathroom doorway. "Ma, you know Emi-lou, she act like one femme with Yvonne, you know," she says. "They sleep close together like boyfriend and girlfriend. And you should see the way Von was rubbing suntan lotion on Emi-lou. Too much, man."

My grandma comes out of the kitchen. She wipes her hands on her golf T-shirt. Luckily, my grandma's been around the block plenty of times. "Shut your mouth, Vicky. Just because you never had no close girlfriends 'cause of your *superb* personality, no talk trash about Emi-lou."

"You wasn't there, Ma," Aunty Vicky says.

"You wouldn't know a friend if she stared you straight in the face," Grandma adds.

"I have eyes. I know what I seen," she says, peeling a red lychee.

"Making something out of nothing," Grandma mutters. "And talk soft. You want Emi-lou to hear this? She already has a hard life."

"She ain't the only one—"

"What?" Grandma says, walking toward her.

"No get me wrong. I not saying it's bad, Ma," Aunty says, popping the glistening white fruit into her mouth. "Plenty girls in this town get girlfriends. So what? I just thought you might want to know, you know, about your beloved Emi-lou-angel-baby. If was one guy all over her, I would tell you just the same."

"She only fourteen, Vicky," Grandma says. "Besides, Louie need one close friend. How would you like Roxanne for a mother and not even know your own father? Anyways, they just kids."

"See, that's the whole trouble with you, Ma. Instead of listening to what I got to say, you give me the whole nine yards. I tell you something 'cause I concerned—eh, I was there."

"Concerned, right," Grandma mutters.

"You never listen to me, Ma," Aunty Vicky says. She sounds sad for a moment. Then she returns to her bitchy self. "I seen how they act. And you told me watch out for the damn kid. Well, I did, and now I telling you. She's acting like one femme."

"Knock it off, Vicky. The two of them like sisters. The Vierras and me, we raised them that way. More than Roxanne will ever be a mother to her or you an aunty, Yvonne will be a friend. I ain't blind. But as far as I can see, I see nothing. They only kids."

"You said that already," Aunty Vicky says, turning on the TV.

My aunty Vicky's the biggest troublemaker. Grandma always says she's the kind of person who values outsiders more than her own family.

My grandma peers in the bathroom door. "No worry," she says. "That orange stuff going fade. You be back to your normal white again. Ho, even your lips burnt orange." She laughs. "Yvonne told me you was on *another* diet so feed you only vegetables. What's that all about?"

"Yeah, another diet. When did Von call?" I ask my grandma.

"Early this morning. And she said you two caddying for Ets and me today as your exercise. Eighteen-hole practice, you know, for the big AJA tournament next weekend. Ets's my partner. Uncle Charlie's coming, too. He the pro, eh? C'mon, get changed."

"I hate diets and I hate sweating," I tell her, but I put on my visor and tennis shoes and turn off the coffeemaker. Sometimes, my grandma forgets. We wait in the garage. Pretty soon, Uncle Charlie, Aunty Etsuko, and Von pull up in the driveway.

"So what's this, Emi-lou, we hear Yvonne going be your trainer?" Uncle says as soon as we get in the car. "Aunty Ets making meatless nishime for dinner now 'cause of you. Gee, I cannot wait to eat." He says this so sassily even Aunty Etsuko tells him to shut up.

Von pinches and twists her daddy's ear and whispers, "No make one big issue out of this before Louie give up, okay?"

"Owee, okay. So solee, nei," Uncle says in his gruff but silly way. "Gomenasai."

I stare out the car window. I think about what I heard my grandma tell Aunty Etsuko on the phone this morning.

"You know, Yvonne is the best friend Emi-lou could ever have. You know how many times I told that girl if she no lose weight, she always going be the laughing-stock. I no like that for her. Not to brag, but all my three girls was lookers, no, Ets? Vicky used to be fat, but she pull down. You tell Yvonne, if she make Emi-lou skinny, she got fifty bucks coming from me. Lord knows we tried everything else already."

"Maybe I fat because you so concerned about my fat," I told my grandma.

"What?" she said, putting her hand over the phone. "You blaming me?"

I didn't answer for a while. "The more you talk about it, the more I want to stay this way." My grandma put the phone down.

"Only because I so concern about you."

"Like when Grandpa use to rag on you about smoking. Only made you smoke more, right?"

"No kidding, rest his soul," she said. "But Emi-lou, I just about ready to do anything to make you lose weight—bribe, beg, scold, pray, anything."

"Then stop ragging on me. I mean, weight is the first thing you talk about whenever you see somebody. 'Ho, Roxanne, you putting on some weight. Wow, Ets, you pulling down. So what, Charlie, eating for two?'"

"I hear you. Just no blame me for your fat," Grandma said.

It hurt me because I hurt her. I didn't mean to lay my fatness on her.

After the long eighteen holes and a Diet Coke at the 19th Hole Bar and Grill, Von says we're going jogging. "But eat a chef salad first, Louie. And only little bit dressing."

"She should put lemon or no dressing at all," Uncle Charlie says.

Von tells him, "I no like Louie to give up so I let her have some good things, too. Ma, tell Dad to stop adding in his two cents about Louie's diet."

"Charlie, my dear," Aunty Etsuko says like she always does when she's getting fed up in a patient way, "squeeze your butt out, *now*. Emi-lou, if you get down to a size seven, I'll take you to JCPenneys. Whatever you want is yours."

"Me, too," Grandma adds in. "I take you shopping. And I *try* stop bugging your ass."

"Me, too," Uncle Charlie says. "But I take you high-class kind shopping at Liberty House."

"Liberty House, for real, Uncle Charlie? Too expensive, that store."

"You deserve the best for being friends with a daughter like mine." Uncle side-eyes Von and makes funny faces at her. "Half-dumb like me, but big heart."

Von tightens her shoe laces, gets up, and starts stretching out. I follow her to the parking lot outside the clubhouse. She's quiet for a long time. "You think you can beat this half-dumb Portagee to that stop sign, or what?" she says.

"You ain't half-dumb, Von, you all smart," I tell her. "One of these days, I going to tell off your father. I know he only kidding, but–"

"I hate it when people make fun of you, too, Louie," Von says. "And you have to lose weight to play softball."

"I on the team 'cause you asked me," I tell her.

"I know. But I like you play for the Astros because you like play," Von says as we walk toward Haihai Street. "I mean, when I played in the pony league with the boys, you couldn't play. Now you can. No do this for me. Do this for you."

"Right," I tell her. "For me. I so fat. If was up to me, I rather take cooking classes at the Y, thank you very much. I doing this for you. I just one big, fat joke."

Von takes my hands and pulls me to follow her up the next hill. We run against the high trades. Then she paces me in a brisk walk back toward the golf course.

"Not if I can help it," she says.

10.
For You, Louie

Von tells me I need to lose the weight fast.

"Why?" I ask her as I take a bite from my third mountain apple.

"They talking," she starts, "they all talking about cutting you from the team, especially Coach Kaaina."

"But I thought I was part of the deal. She promised Uncle Charlie."

Von looks away from me. "Promises–"

"Made to be broken?"

"Eh, you talk clichés, too," Von says as she tries to lighten me up. She tosses me another apple.

"Get serious, Von," I scold. "Not fair."

"You know, and I know, that once you set you mind to something, you do it come hell or high tide. You strong enough for me and you." Von puts me in a headlock and noogies my hair. "So for the rest of this summer, you best be doing things my way."

"You shame of me, Von?" I ask out of nowhere.

"Shame?" She laughs. "No be silly."

"Then what the real reason you like me lose weight?"

"So you can stay on the team," Von says as she shuffles her feet on the cold cement floor of the garage.

"C'mon, Von," I tell her, "I know you better than you know yourself."

"I cannot stand it," she says at last, "when people look at you and the first thing they see is your fat ass, Louie. I like them see the real you, the one I know. I no like you be the joke. I no like you be in pain. You my best girl, my best friend," she says, punching my arm.

We sit on the back porch of Grandma's house. I take a deep breath. "Okay," I tell her at last.

"You lose twenty pounds by September."

"Twenty?"

"You heard me." Von brushes a mosquito away from my face. "The buck stop right here." She says this with conviction. "The vegetables and running ain't enough," she says as she pulls out a small steno tablet from her pocket.

"I hate those multivitamins from Longs," I tell her. "They make me burp all day long. The apples and watermelon, raw sunflower seeds from the hippie health store–they make me gassy." I watch Von's eyes widen.

"You gotta stop eating, Louie."

"What?"

"Starve and sweat," she says.

"No way. I give up," I tell her. "Quit. Pau. Kaput. Let me know when you come up with the real plan." Even though I protest, somehow when Von talks about making me skinny, I know it can happen.

Von writes in her steno tablet:

Morning/Tennis

Afternoon/softball practice

Ride bike everyplace, including Carvalho Park.

Maybe I can do this, I think. I look up from Von's list. She's smiling at me as she presses her warm leg to mine.

"We have to step up the Von-starve-and-sweat plan," she says with a grin. "Just follow me."

Von and I ride our bikes instead of taking the sampan bus all the way to downtown Hilo. I follow her along the muggy side streets. The summer heat broils the browning lawns. Stray dogs lumber sideways looking for shade. She locks our bikes together outside of Hilo Drugs.

Von peers down the cool, musty aisles of the old drugstore. "We have to do it my way, Louie," Von says. "Starve and sweat." She reaches for the dusty boxes of time-release appetite suppressants, turquoise-colored diuretics, mint, chocolate, and fruit-flavored laxatives.

"But, this is drugs," I tell her as I start to walk away. "I ain't doing this crap. I ain't anorexic."

"Louie," she hisses as she grabs my arm. "You starve for one week, flush out your system, then I let you rest. Then you starve again. Meantime, you exercise every day." Her eyes search the round mirrors near the ceiling for the old Japanese woman who works the register.

"What you thinking, Von? You better not steal. I get money," I tell her. The woman in the mirror perks up as she tries to locate the whispering. "You promise you never shoplifting again."

Because we never had enough money to get things for each other, it wasn't stealing, we used to rationalize. All the things we stole were actually small gifts to each other.

I'd hold a tube of mascara in Payless. She'd shoplift it. The next day, I'd find it in my purse.

She'd look at a Cecilio & Kapono cassette at MJS. I'd steal it. The next day, she'd find it in her backpack.

We stopped after being dragged to the store manager's office in Sears. He emptied our pockets. Nothing was there.

"I threw the ring in Women's," Von said to me as we were escorted from the mall by security.

Von peers down the aisle in Hilo Drugs. "But ten bucks ain't enough," she whispers as she takes the money from my hand. "We going pay for as much as we can, so it ain't really a five-finger discount." She places several boxes in my backpack.

"If my grandma ever found out about this . . . and if she knew I was taking pills . . . and if we get caught shoplifting again—"

Von places her hand over my mouth. "We never got caught." She motions with her other hand, and I walk with her toward the front of the store. My feet don't feel the ground. My heart pounds visibly through my clothes. My breath feels shallow. I feel light-headed and blurry-eyed. Blood drains from my face. Everything moves in slow motion.

Von puts our boxes on the counter. She scratches her nose and bites her lip.

"Ten dollars and fifty-eight cents. Will this be all?" the old lady asks Von.

"Yup," Von says, handing her the ten.

"Fifty-eight cents, please," the old lady says narrowing her gaze on Von's trembling hand.

"Oh," Von says reaching into her pocket, "right, you said fifty-eight cents." She spills some loose change all over the counter.

I step up to the counter and confidently count out thirty-five cents. "I got some more change in my backpack," I tell the lady. I reach into the side pocket and pull out a quarter. I snap it on the counter. "Thank you for the patience," I tell her. "Keep the change."

Von shakes her head. "Cool, cucumber," she says, nudging me in the back and following me out the door.

11.
The Third Leg

The girls on the team start helping me out with the Von-starve-and-sweat plan. Rae Kalani, our team captain, says, "I like play tennis with you guys tomorrow morning. Where you play, Von, Lincoln Park? I be there."

Her pretty friend Anita lights a cigarette for Rae and laughs. "See how Rae acts innocent," she tells Chooch. "She played first singles for the Kohala Cowboys." Anita's always with Rae at practice and at parties. And she never treats me like a wanna-be. "You're looking good, Louie," she says, "to me, you're fine."

"Not fine enough," Von says.

I look at my feet then steal a stink-eye at Von.

"At least she trying, Von," Rae says as she sits down next to Anita. "Her legs and ass getting smaller."

"Not small enough," Von says.

"Lighten up, bully," Anita tells her.

All of them talking about my body makes me feel weird. But it also feels weirdly wonderful to be the center of attention. I know some of the other girls think Von's too tough on me, but I know Von's doing this for my own good. I could never do this alone.

"Louie?" Anita says. "You all right with this?"

"Whatever," I tell her. "If Von says I get more to go—"

"Oh, jeez," Rae says, "you giving her big head. C'mon, Von, you Richard Simmons wanna-be, let me pop your bubble. Three sets?"

"I like be your partner, Rae," Chooch says. "We clean these puppies up. Eh, Babes, why no come play tennis with us? You should diet with Louie. Girl, you huffing around the plates with some thunder in those thighs, man."

Babes says nothing. She just looks me over, up and down. "Why, I could be skinny in no time if Von was my trainer, too." She smirks.

Von gives Babes a smile she never did smile at me.

"Shoots," Von says, "come pick us up at Louie's house tomorrow morning."

My face flushes uncomfortably. I think about what Uncle Charlie said about butchies. But Von is not a butchie. And she'll never be one. Not if I can do something about it. Why can't Babes just butt out?

"But . . . " I stammer.

"But what?" Von challenges me.

"Whatever you say, Von," I say softly.

"Better be," she says.

I stare her down and she finally lowers her eyes.

My aunty Vicky watches us closely. She glances at Babes and Von, then quickly looks back at me. She wants to tell my grandma how we're acting, so I try really hard to make my face blank.

"C'mon, Von," I say, grabbing her by the elbow, "we have to bike home before come dark and your father yell at us. Poker night, tonight, you know."

"Oh, yeah. We go, Louie." Von starts to take the lock off of our bikes.

"Throw your bikes in the back of my truck 'cause getting dark already," Babes says with concern. She moves closer to Von. "So what you doing tonight?" she asks. "Like go cruising with me, Kyle, and Sterling? He coming in from Pāhoa."

I don't look at Von. I just think of Kyle and I get this good but funny feeling in my bones. He's the cutest thing you've ever seen with light ehu hair, light brown eyes, golden biceps, and no pimples on his face. I don't tell anyone, not even Von, that I don't care what he said to me that day at Hāpuna Beach. He didn't mean it. It was a *joke* and everybody took him wrong.

"Then we can meet the girls down at Wailoa," Babes continues. "They drinking tonight."

I give Von the look. She's supposed to be able to read my thoughts. But Babes distracts her. So I give Von a real stink-eye and grit my teeth. "We don't drink, Yvonne, remember?"

"You no need drink," Babes says. "But if you one of us, then you party with us. Big baby," Babes says to me, "this not the Sesame Street softball league. So what, Von, you like come?"

"Shoots," Von says. She playfully shoves me away but

47

I lose my balance and fall on the grass. Anita helps me up off the ground.

"Hey now, no internal strife," Rae scolds. "We see you tonight. Anita, where my keys? We get some more soda in the cooler? Von and Babes, you ain't drinking, you hear me?"

"Louie, you sit with me," Anita says. "I only drink Seven Up," she whispers in my ear.

"Yeah," Babes mutters. "Go sit with Aunty Anita. She your best friend Rudy Rudman's aunty, right?" Anita nods.

"Von my best friend," I tell Babes.

Babes nods her head slowly and sarcastically, looking me straight in the eye. Von shakes her head at me. Every time we're around Babes, which has been every day since we joined the Hilo Astros, it gets harder and harder. They get closer. The talk softly, so I can't hear them.

"V-a-L, right, Von?" She's looking at Babes. "Right?"

"Huh? You said something, Louie?"

12.
Nobody Fat

This body Von creates for me through starvation, pep talks, fistfuls of pills, sweat, mind-over-matter, and exercise is not mine. All of a sudden, there's nothing between me and the world.

So-and-so hates me because I'm fat. I suck at softball because I'm fat. I choke because I'm fat. I'm unpopular because I'm fat. I have no boyfriend because I'm fat. I never get invited to cool parties, sleep-overs, social clubs, or dances because I'm fat.

I live with my grandma and an aunty Vicky with a bad attitude because I'm fat. Roxanne hates me because I'm fat. I have no father because I'm fat.

I'm nobody. I'm fat. The end.

Now what? I'm not fat. So it must be me. But who am I, if not Emi-oink?

I try not to think about it too much. I can't. The pills make me jittery all the time. I'm constantly knocking things off of the kitchen counter. My heart races and skips beats. My eyes dart about quickly. My mind never quiets. I can't fall asleep at night.

It feels funny getting skinny, not seeing my thighs spread out over the sticky car seat, having knuckles in my hands, a visible collarbone. I'm scared, but I don't tell Von or anybody. They might think I'm ungrateful—that they helped me get skinny and now I can't handle it.

And Von always says she's the tough outward and I'm the tough inward for all that I've had to go through in fourteen years.

"Tough inward?" I ask her.

Von imitates my voice. "Von, sit down. You can pass this damn social studies test if you dig deep. Von, even if your father grounded you for two weeks, you always remember that you got a good daddy. Von, if I told you once, I told you ten million times—you not half-stupid, you all smart," she says with a tender smile.

"I don't feel like me—" I stop. After that tough inward speech, I don't want her to think me weak, no longer the Louie who can take things, explain things, and understand things for both of us.

The morning of my back-to-school shopping spree, I wake up and stumble in the hallway. I hear my grandma's voice pulling me like a rope that thins, then disappears. I hit my head on the moulding.

When I open my eyes, I see the ceiling. "Emi-lou? You fainted. You damn kid, you better eat something, now." She shoves a piece of English muffin in my mouth. I spit it out onto the floor.

"Too much butter," I manage to say. "Von said no fat and no carbs this week."

"You come to the table and have breakfast right now," she says, yanking me to my feet. "I no like you get sick."

"Von said no," I tell her.

"She rule your body? What *you* got to say about that?"

"Nothing."

"You want me to tell Aunty Ets to cancel our back-to-school shopping?"

"No."

Grandma pushes me toward the dining room table. She serves me a small bowl of hot rice with scrambled eggs. "You better be moderate with this diet thing. Pass me a pen from your purse," Grandma says. "I need to write a list." She reaches for my bag.

The pills are all in my bag. I snatch it away from her.

"Whatever you got in there, Emi-lou," she says, "you better tell me about it. Your mother was your age when she started lying to me about everything. You remember I always say that little white lies are lies all the same."

Von comes in the back door. "C'mon," she says to us. "The mall's jamming."

13.
Final Touches

Aunty Etsuko, Grandma, Von, and I move like whirlwinds through JCPenney. Bongo, Mossimo, Guess, Levi, and Esprit–package after package of clothes and accessories. Von gets lots of stuff too for being the best trainer–flannel shirts, Levis, and Nikes. Uncle Charlie waits impatiently.

The strangest part for me is having all the clothes fit and fit right. Normally, Grandma has to get three different sizes, tug and pull, grumble and push me in front of the mirror and complain about how I have to stop eating like a maniac pig. We usually find only one or two outfits at the most that look halfway okay.

This time she says, "You look so nice, Emi-lou. Oh, no! What we going choose? You look so good in everything."

I look at myself in the mirror. I still feel like me. I still see the same me. How come everybody's seeing some-body else? I was nobody fat. Am I somebody skinny?

"Can you imagine what a change this girl made?"

Aunty Etsuko says. "We're so proud of you, Emi-lou. You're a whole new person."

My eyes are the same.

"And she looks just like Roxanne," Aunty Etsuko adds. "Let's go to the cosmetics counter next." Just like my mother? It's enough to make me want to eat. Or puke.

"We go wait outside, Yvonne," Uncle Charlie tells her. "You not into this, eh? Ets, get Yvonne one of those black dresses. And buy her some lipstick, too."

"Nah, pass," Von mutters as she nudges me. "Make sure they forget, eh, Louie." I nod.

"Can't be having no truck driver in man clothes for a daughter, right, Ets?" Uncle Charlie pats the empty bench and motions for Von to join him.

"She ain't," I tell him. He looks surprised. "Stop saying that kine stuff. Just leave her alone."

"Okay, okay, just kidding. I give up," Uncle Charlie says, raising both hands.

I turn toward the dressing room mirror. Like I said, it feels funny looking at my face, the angles sharp and the chin pointed. And everybody we see says something about my body. That feels funny, too, like their eyes are all over me.

Judith Wong, my ex-friend, social-ladder climber, now one of the popular Jap-girls, sees me. "Is that you, Emi-lou?"

"No, it's Emi-fat, eat a rat, remember?" I tell her. Von crosses her arms, tilts back her head, and nods slowly.

"Oh please, Emi, I never said those things."

"Not to my face," I tell her.

"Well, I'm a bigger person than that," she says.

"Bigger is right." Von laughs.

"See you at school," she says as her friends sashay away with her.

"I no think so," I yell.

"So much for famous last words." Von laughs.

After shopping, Von and I decide to spend the last two days before school doing the final touches. She takes a couple of beers from her refridge and we climb onto the tin roof of her house where it's August-hot.

"Beer's a good conditioner, you know," she says. She pours half of it on my hair and I pour the rest on her hair. We share the other bottle. The buzz makes me giddy. "I was reading *Teen* magazine in my father's office," Von says, "and something make me turn to Genevieve. So anyway, I ask her, 'Eh, Viva, how you got your hair all ehu like that?' And she tell, 'I put Sun-In and lemon juice before I go down Four Miles. Come all orange like this.'"

"Viva's hair look real nice," I tell Von.

"You like try, Louie?"

"I do anything you say, you know that, Von. Look, you made me skinny."

"No give me that. You and me know that I yank your chain and order your ass around, but when push come to shove, you strong right here," Von says as she places her clenched fist at the pit of her gut. "So, you trust me, right?"

I look at my small wrists and my long fingers. I nod.

She sprays Sun-In on my hair. Then she squeezes the lemon juice in her hands before rubbing it on my hair.

I sit between her legs and she combs my hair nicely, not like my mother when I was a little girl, pulling and yanking hard. Von combs my hair till I close my eyes, it feels so warm up there. Von's soft hands on my hair as we sit on the tin roof of her house.

14.

Deeper Than the Deep Blue Sea

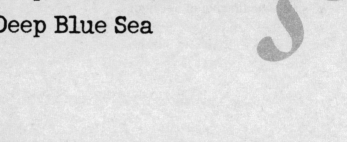

The sun through my curtains, I hear the chickens outside and smell the puakenikeni in bloom. The first day of school's not like any other school day. I get up pretty cheerfully, my eyes full of light.

I wash my hair and my face. Brush my teeth with a lilting smile. My clothes are ironed and hanging on the doorknob, my sandals waiting by the door. A new bag's slung over the back of a dining room chair. And I'm even waiting for my grandma *before* she finishes her coffee.

But this only happens for the first week. Thereafter, I push the snooze button three times. I can never decide what to wear. I can't find my bag and Grandma's tooting the horn as I stumble out the door.

My grandma rinses her mug and gives me the start-of-a-new-year lecture. "You starting off with a clean slate. Make the best of this year. This your last year in intermediate, so make it count. You gotta be"—this next part I can repeat by heart—"the best that you can be."

She drops Von and me off at the intermediate school campus, which is next to the high school campus. I hurry Von toward the office so we can find our homeroom teachers. Von pulls me the other way.

"Where we going?" I ask her.

"Babes said to meet her at the A-building bathroom," Von tells me. "They all sit on the steps outside."

"You not hanging out at the shop bathroom this year?"

"No," Von says as she picks up her step. "C'mon, Louie."

"I told Rudy I was meeting him outside the student gov room. I cannot dog him, you know." I turn to head back to our campus.

"The volleyball boys hang out with Babes them." I stop. Von doesn't mention Kyle's name. But I never talk to her about Babes, either. And I get a strong feeling that the way I feel about Kyle is the way Von feels about Babes.

We analyze everything else in our lives. And if we get real deep, way inside, Von always knows how to make light of it. She says, "Whoa, Louie-Louie, now that's deep, deeper than the deep blue sea." And after a moment of silence, we bust out laughing even if the subject was dead serious.

So I follow Von to the A-building bathroom. They all look sharp in their new school clothes. "Eh, Happy New Year!" Babes yells as all the girls laugh. "So what, Von, who your date?" she asks. I must look dorky in my JCPenney dress. She wants everybody to look and stare. "What you did to your hair, man?"

"No act, Louie look good," Von says. Kyle turns his head. He doesn't say anything but I feel his eyes on my body, my hair golden and smooth. Von even put a puakenikeni flower behind my ear this morning. She catches Kyle looking at me. "What, brah, where the fat white whale?"

Kyle doesn't say a word at first. Then, "Howzit, Von, long time no see. What you guys doing up the high school campus? You only ninth grade."

"Babes told us where to meet you guys. Beef with your cuz, Cuz," Von says to Kyle.

"Cool your jets, Kyle," Genevieve Ching says. "Eh, Louie, nice hair. Von told you where she got her hair-dressing lessons?" Viva laughs, because now I look just like her.

I look toward the steps where all the volleyball boys hang out. "How come Sterling stay here?" I whisper to Von.

"His mother cannot handle him," Von tells me, "so she sent him from Pāhoa to get straighten out by his grandma."

It's like he knows we're talking about him. He walks over. "Howzit, Von," Sterling says and they low-five each other. "Hey, Louie. That's you? You ate only air sandwich since I last seen you or what?" Sterling gives me a hug like a brother.

"You living with Coach Kaaina?" I ask him.

"Grams," he laughs, "is way more strict than my moms."

"I know how that is," I tell him.

"Von told me your grandma been raising you, that's true?"

"Yeah, but she no spoil me like most grandmas," I tell him. "But she all right. Better than my mother. Ask Von."

"I did, I mean, ask Von about—" he stumbles. "I mean, my grams kick ass, too. And my mother sound like yours."

"Maybe we should share notes," I tell him and he laughs. I realize that everybody's staring at Sterling and the dork having a conversation. I start feeling self-conscious and embarrassed. I look at my watch. "Oh, no, Von," I blurt out. "We better run back to the inter-mediate side before the tardy bell ring."

"Catch you first recess, Von," Babes says and they look at each other. "Like drag?" she asks Von and holds out her cigarette. Babes is real ballsy, smoking out in the open. She hides it behind her back, though, when one of the math teachers walks up the stairway.

"Come back with Von," Sterling says to me before I leave. "All us just hang—"

"Yeah, no forget your shadow," Babes tells Von.

"Yeah, your used-to-be fat ass shadow." Kyle laughs.

"I ain't her shadow, you, you—" I start, as Von pushes me toward the intermediate campus.

15.
So What, Louie, You Smart?

Von and I have homeroom and first period right next to each other. When we get there, I look inside her room. She has Algebra I with smart-looking gifted and talented types—Japanese, haole, and Chinese kids.

I look inside my class, Mathematics II. I think I'm in the medium class. "See Von, you smart in math," I tell her and she gives me the head jerk, *check you laters*. She looks bad as she walks in the class with all the dorks.

We don't share too many classes after that except home ec and P.E. Von tells me that she has dumb social studies and medium English. I tell her that I have high social studies and high English. Von's taking advanced sports II for her elective and I'm taking newswriting. I have to walk over to the high school campus for this class.

After our P.E. class, Von says, "I meet you by the A-building bathroom after school, since you on the high school side anyway."

"Okay," I tell her, "but hurry up 'cause my grandma going get mad if we not at the ramp by two-forty-five."

In newswriting class, there aren't very many students. I sit down in the front and try to be inconspicuous. Only three intermediate interns are selected for this class every year and they're usually from gifted and talented English class.

This year, the teachers pick Jenni Takatani, g/t in all subjects except P.E., the biggest tightwad with answers, and the ugliest permed hair. Von hates her. In last year's hoss elections, she was the Girl Most Likely to Succeed and Most Intellectual.

Their second pick was Nancy Nitta, who's nice for a square Jap with an organizational sense to rival the anal among us. Nancy won the Woman of the Century national essay contest and a free trip to Washington, D.C., for her great-great-grandma's story of immigrating to America from Japan only to work for a dollar a day on a sugar plantation in Hawai'i but still embrace freedom and the Constitution.

Them two. And me.

I *think* I deserve to be in this class. I've been a pretty good English student, but not the best. It did cross my mind that my grandma, a retired schoolteacher, could've influenced the decision. And fat or no fat, I feel uncomfortable being here. My ex-friend Judith Wong, voted Most Artistic Girl and Most Creative, should've been here. I never won a hoss election or a major award like Jenni, Judith, or Nancy. I've never been considered for the gifted and talented program. The only thing I've ever had in common with them was a bad perm.

When the tardy bell rings, all the high school students stagger in late. "Welcome to another year," Mrs. Hatayama, the young newswriting advisor, tells the class. "All of you returnees, you know what you're in for." They all moan and groan. "And a fond aloha to our interns from the intermediate campus right here in the front." The class laughs because we look like three scared mice sitting in the front row. A few more students trail in the back door.

"Which of you is Nancy Nitta?"

Nancy makes a small motion raising her hand. "Here."

"And Jenni Takatani?"

She has no shame. She turns around as she waves and exclaims, "Present."

"And finally, Emi-lou Kaya."

Before I can even say here, present, gifted and talented, somebody says, "Hey, Louie."

And then another sarcastic voice pipes in, "Hey, *Louie*? Hatayama said her name Emi-lou, let's not forget it." I turn around and see Sterling. He gives me a head-jerk hi. Kyle sits tilting his chair in the back of the room. He's surrounded by student gov girls.

For the rest of the period, Kyle acts like he doesn't even know me. Sterling sits next to him. It looks sort of like male bonding. One good thing is that their acknowledgment of me makes me the most-esteemed intern. But big deal.

On the way to A-building bathroom after the bell rings, Kyle catches up to me. I catch major thrills. "So what, Louie, you smart?" he asks.

"Maybe," I tell him. "Maybe not."

"Be a pal and help me write all, I mean, some of my stories for me, okay?" he asks with that boyish grin, dimples, white teeth, light brown eyes, and ehu hair.

"Maybe," I tell him as I continue walking. "You treat me like dirt. Why should I?" Sterling catches up to us.

"You'll do it," he whispers, "for me."

"Do what?" Sterling asks.

"Nothing, brah," Kyle says, giving me a secret look to shut my mouth. And I do because I love the intimacy of it all.

I'm happy that Kyle even walks side by side with me out of the classroom, where everybody, all the titas and student gov people in our newswriting class, hang out. They all see me—that ninth grader, her, the size seven, the girl with highlighted hair, skinny Emi-lou Kaya—walking with Kyle Kiyabu.

"Yeah, okay. Whatevers," I tell him.

Sterling looks at me then at Kyle. He shakes his head and lights a cigarette.

But I don't care. I'm walking with Kyle Kiyabu, middle blocker, boys volleyball, Big Island champs, changing the subject fast so that by the time we get to the A-building bathroom where Von's waiting, she doesn't know what Kyle asked. And she doesn't know what I answered.

16.

The Japanese Say
Bad Luck Comes in Threes

This, I believe.

Number one starts with everybody thinking the Hilo Astros are guaranteed to take the district play-offs in the Big Island Women's Softball Tournament.

But something seems wrong with the team. Von's in a slump all weekend. She's the number three batter—she's supposed to be a reliable hitter. And we make lots of unforced errors, especially Viva, Babes, and me. All the young ones keep screwing up.

Aunty Vicky starts making cracks like, "Bench um, Aunty Erma. See, we should've gotten rid of Emi-lou and brought in Crimson and Mary Ann. Sheez, we came to win or what? Dammit, this is suppose to be easy."

The dugout feels tense all the time. And when the Waiākea Uka Alapas beat the Kaūmana Krew, they take the top spot with a clean record. Coach Kaaina tells all the girls to be in attendance at the game between Kaūmana Krew and Pana'ewa Puakea.

If the Krew wins, they tie with us for second and we play off for second spot. "You make me so mad," she yells. "Playing like one inexperience team—throwing to the wrong bases, not hitting the cut-off man. That's all stupid errors. The runner tagging up and you throwing all over the damn place."

"Scout for their weak spots," Rae Kalani tells us. "Watch how on the left side of the field, the Krew get all their strong players. Watch what happen when you go the other way."

"Their pitcher shooting on the inside of the plate," Choochie tells us in her calm way, "so that you force to hit to the left side of field. Think."

"I swear," Coach Kaaina says, "you girls better be watching good."

The Krew blows out the Puakeas. Both the Hilo Astros and the Kaūmana Krew scout the game between the Alapas and the Hilo Homestead.

All of us sit glumly in the stands—Rae, Choochie, Viva, Babes, and Aunty Vicky, who sits with Kyle Kiyabu. Sterling's there, too, with Coach Kaaina, her face harsh and mad. Von and I sit with Anita and Rudy near the rest of them. Von looks bummed out.

"If you go to the hot dog stand," I tell her, "I treat you three hot dogs." She's hungry because she hasn't eaten since breakfast, and it's past dinnertime already.

"Get a Seven Up for Rae and Rudy," Anita tells Von.

"Okay, and I bring you a Diet Coke and pretzels, okay, Louie?" she says. "Pretzels ain't fried in fat. You can share with Rudy." She's still starving me every other day. And she's still stealing pills for me. I don't know how much longer I can take it, but at least it's kept me on the team till the play-offs.

After Von leaves, somebody starts swearing behind me and kicks my bag off the bleachers. I bend down to see where it went and something hits me in the head. I turn to see one of the Mahina twins from St. Joseph's who plays off-season for the Krew. We have a long-standing, crosstown double rivalry: St. Joe's hates Hilo High, and the Krew hates the Astros and vice versa. It's Gina Mahina who kicked my bag.

JoJo Mahina, her other half says, "Good for her."

"Go get your bag," Gina whispers in my ear, "you bench-warming lez." She sticks her feet under my ass and pushes my back.

"Stop it," Rudy snaps.

"You stop it, faggot," Gina says, her loose wrist flapping. Anita stands up.

I don't see Von coming until she strides up the bleachers, grabs Anita and me by the arms, and moves us to the bottom. "Sit right here," she tells me. "Rudy, get down here and watch the food." Then Von climbs back up the stands.

The Mahina twins sit together, smirking but trying to ignore Von. "Eh, Gina, go pick up my friend's bag," Von tells her.

"Her girlfriend's bag," JoJo mutters. "Get it yourself."

"What?" Von asks, stepping up to JoJo. Gina shoves Von hard in the chest, not once, but twice. So Von shoves her back. The three of them start swinging. Rae and Choochie get up as somebody from the Krew pushes Babes from behind. Then Babes gets crazy mad.

Sterling climbs up the bleachers and grabs Von. Gina Mahina hits Von in the face and her mouth starts bleeding. He drags her to the bottom of the stands.

"They going disqualify your team," Huggie Kaaina tells his wife.

"Knock it off," Coach Kaaina yells, making her way up the bleachers.

Pretty soon, the cops come and clear the crowd.

Uncle Charlie, Aunty Etsuko, and Grandma come running toward us. "Yvonne," Uncle Charlie calls. "What the hell's going on? Gunfunnit, you girls have no sportsmanship."

"Daddy, you don't know—" Von starts.

"Get down here, now," he yells in front of all the jeering spectators.

"She pushed Von first," I tell Uncle Charlie.

"Her name is *Yvonne*!" he yells. "You got that, Emilou?" he says, as he flicks my head then paddles my butt.

Sterling's still holding Von. Kyle starts laughing at all of us.

"What's so funny, asshole?" Von tells him.

"That's enough, Yvonne," Uncle Charlie says.

"I seen you laughing and clapping, brah, what's with that?" Von's not going to let this one go. She looks at Babes. In this moment, Von should've read her. She would've known everything she needed to know about her. Blood runs thicker than water. "You wait, Kyle," Von goes on as she steps toward him.

"Yvonne! You stop now!" Aunty Etsuko yells and Von doesn't answer.

Von couldn't play in the rubber match game between the Hilo Astros and the Kaūmana Krew. Uncle Charlie grounded her as soon as he got us in the car. The Hilo Astros still won.

And all the way home that evening, Von stared out the car window and said nothing to me, nothing about Kyle, nothing about Babes, nothing at all.

17.
Rudy Rudman

I have been friends with Rudy Rudman since the seventh grade because Von decided to smoke cigarettes, shoot craps, and pitch quarters in a daily game of digit with the rugged titas and stoned-out mokes in the shop bathroom.

Thank God I found a new friend. It was *like* at first sight because when our eyes met in the crowded clarinet section, me buried five-deep with the second clarinets, and Rudy in the second seat, first clarinet section, I knew we would be friends. And Von always liked him.

"Soul mates, dahling," he often said. "I read our numbers."

Once in a while, Von would spend a recess with Rudy and me, just to remind the rest of the school that we had a backer and they better not harass us. So they never harassed us in front of her, just behind her back.

Rudy Rudman decided on a whim to run for Hilo Intermediate's student body president. He begged for me to be his campaign manager. "I know you ain't the limelight type, let alone the student gov groupie the rest of these unqualified candidates are, but Louie, as a friend, just help me win."

"How you going win?" I asked. "I mean—"

"Listen, girl, we bust our tiny little glutes, you create all my clever slogans and posters with that fertile mind of yours—"

"And?"

"And I usher the two of us into the world of the mega-involved," he said with a flourish of large circles with his arms and snaps.

"Why?"

"We can't be social pariahs all our lives, right, girlfriend? You just follow Uncle Rudy, who is ultra-magnifico, generoso with the spotlight."

I had to laugh. "C'mon, dude, be real. How you going win?"

He answered very matter-of-factly. "We make Von strong-arm my votes with those barbarian friends of hers." Rudy snapped twice, fired an imaginary pistol, then blew off the invisible smoky discharge.

"Now you talking," I told him as we high-fived.

So I created his slogans and posters. "Get in the Mood, Vote for Rude," and "Shake your Boo-dee, Vote for Rudy." My best was, "Only the Crude Vote for Jude, but the In-Dude Votes for Rude." Judith Wong didn't stand a chance with her "You Can't Go Wrong with Wong" posters. And once Von and her tita and moke friends made it known that they backed Rudy, she was toast.

"It pays to have the underworld on your side," Rudy boasted when the elections committee announced the results over the p.a. system.

For our back-to-school pep rally, he dimmed all the lights in the caf, boogied on the stage to "Raspberry Beret" in a pink Lycra jumpsuit showing every bodily bump, with a pink beret on his head–then he sang "Memories, All Alone in the Moonlight" in a falsetto, a cappella voice after which he delivered an inspirational cry for school spirit and personal involvement. The titas and mokes hana-houed Rudy, so no one dared to laugh at him.

Then he proceeded to drag my unspirited, unpopular, but now size-seven glutes to the center of student activities. "The handsome and spirited king needs a gorgeous and vivacious queen," he whispered to me at our first float planning meeting. "Or vice versa, honey."

Then the second bad luck comes.

For the Aloha Week parade this year, the Hilo Intermediate student council decides to build a float. It's a last-minute decision voted upon in an emergency student gov meeting, but Rudy wants to show the high school that we have spirit, too.

Usually the intermediate school does nothing. They barely scrape up a graduation dance at the end of the year. This according to Von, who thinks my participation in student gov activities is stupid; student gov is full of babies, dorks, the uncool; a waste of time, phony, elitist; a bunch of ass-kissing wanna-bes.

"You sure we can do this float thing?" I ask Rudy.

"There's only two words in the Book of Rudy—can and do, dahling, so continue to draw, sketch, and design our float plan," he orders me, flicking his wrist in my face. "Go on, go on, don't let my glamour stop you."

"You shoulda made nice to Judith Wong after the election," I scold him. "See, now she all uncooperative."

"Most Artistic Girl ain't never going be Miss Gracious Loser, the pout-face trout. Lucky thing I got you, babe," he says as he breaks out into a Sonny and Cher song. "'Cause you're the best thing, that ever happen to me," he sings.

"I get it," I tell him.

"It's always the woman behind the man," Rudy says as he rubs my back.

"Woman behind the woman," I tell him.

"Ooohhh, meee-ow," he says, hissing at me with his hand turned claw.

So I draw and sketch a whole afternoon in the student gov office. But even so, Rudy and I manage to create the ugliest float in the history of the Aloha Week parade.

The chicken wire bends wrong and nails barely hold together rotting scraps of lumber. We run out of tissue paper to make flowers to put on the chicken wire so we start using toilet paper flowers tinged with red lipstick until Jenni Takatani, student gov secretary, mentions that this is an *Aloha Week* float. The four of us building the damn thing panic because we haven't put a single real flower on the whole float.

So we pick staghorn fern from Kaūmana and start sticking the stems in the chicken wire. We pick torch ginger, plumeria, and anthuriums that Rudy Rudman,

Traci Miyahara (the useless v.p.), Darla Wong (the treasurer, Judith's cousin, who could hardly count and was in lower math than me), and I have growing in our yards. Our float looks real Portagee-alcoholic-makeup-artist-sniffing-fingernail-polish-remover-and-white-out terrible.

It's Rudy's idea to fashion papier-mâché giant heads of menehune, the intermediate school mascot. "Cute, yeah, Louie, these little elf-things," he says pointing at a menehune drawing in one of our library books. "They look like little Hawaiian Santa's helpers."

"Whatever."

"Enthusiasm, girl, let's see some."

His last minute brainstorm involves four menehune shaking hands to represent the seventh graders, eighth graders, ninth graders, and the faculty. And if they still don't get it, he has us make labels. We paint 7TH, 8TH, 9TH, AND FAC. across the menehune's foreheads. The theme for our float, cardboard letters covered with tin foil and purple cellophane is: UNITY: 7TH 8TH 9TH GRADERS HILO INT. STYLE.

"What about the faculty?" I ask. "In the theme?"

"They get it, girlfriend. I mean, they get college degree, sheez. Let's not get all literal," he says. "Are you with me?"

Nobody answers, their hands too tired from cutting out letters from huge pieces of washing machine cardboard with crappy school scissors. We had already finished all four menehune heads, and after all that hard labor, were not about to throw one into the proverbial scrap heap.

On the day of the parade, I have to admit, I feel kind of proud. Von hadn't come around, but somehow, student gov seemed like an okay thing for me. We had worked all night to make the parade deadline. The four boys who volunteer to wear the malos with the papier-mâché giant menehune heads arrive at Rudy's garage.

Rudy acts bossy as he dresses Dennis Kawachi. "You too damn skinny for a menehune," he grumbles. "Push out your pidgeon chest."

Yun Pui Chock. "You too damn too Northern Chinesy handsome for a menehune, so uglify yourself right now."

Raleigh Rubianes. "You too damn fat and black, but nothing we can do about genetics, honey."

And Randall Hiyoto. "Squat your ass down. You too tall for a menehune."

They have a hard time holding the heavy papier-mâché heads on their own heads while shaking hands in UNITY. They fall off balance and the menehune heads start clunking into each other on the float when the truck moves. Worse yet, with every stop and go, they get thrown off balance and a couple of the menehune eye holes move to face the wrong direction.

Uncle Charlie, Aunty Ets, Grandma, and Von drop me off at Rudy's garage. "We meet you by the Dairy Queen on Waianuenue Ave.," Von says to me.

"Rudy said I could ride in the front of the truck," I tell her.

"Wow, big thrills, Louie-Louie," she says as they drive off.

74

"It is to me," I yell. I don't think she heard me.

The parade route's not so long and Rudy lets me stand on the iron grille foot stand outside the door of the truck. I'm pretty cool, I think to myself—skinny, tinted-haired me hanging on to the side of the truck and waving at little kids along the parade route.

When we turn the corner of Waianuenue Avenue, I see Von, Grandma, Aunty Vicky, and Uncle Charlie.

"Emi-lou, look our way," Aunty Ets says as she snaps a picture of me on the float.

"Emi-lou, you look stupid, you geek," Aunty Vicky yells as Grandma tries to give her a slap.

Babes stands by Von. She must've picked up Aunty Vicky.

"Hi, Von. See, Grandma, turned out nice. Hi, Uncle. Hi, Aunty Ets." I wave as I pose for another shot. I leave out Babes and Aunty Vicky on purpose since I am commanding center stage here.

"Nice, your float," Grandma says. Even if my float looks ugly, she knows how hard I'd been working on it.

"Jump off, Louie," Von yells. "We go drink Mr. Misty at Dairy Queen. I treat you."

I nod, then poise myself to jump.

"No jump, Louie," Randall Hiyoto warns me through his papier-mâché mouth.

I stick my tongue out at him and laugh. "Laters, chumps," I tell them in an attempt to look like the cool chick able to abandon ship for a Mr. Misty with rugged friends.

And then, I jump. But I don't tell my feet to keep moving because the truck's still moving, you know, momentum, forward motion and all that. I just jump.

My feet stick to the road. I fall forward right on my face. My forehead hits the asphalt and I start rolling on the slippery street. I nearly get trampled by the horseback riders behind us. I get strawberry cuts on my forehead and both knees, the little kids and clowns on foot laughing.

I want to bury my face in the gutter and die. Bad luck number two.

Meanwhile, Rudy's yelling, enunciating his syllables, "Roll some more, Lou-wee, roll out of the way, girlfriend! Get more horses coming!"

The guys on the float laugh so hard, their papier-mâché heads bounce and clunk into each other. Von runs out onto the road, picks me up, and dusts me off.

Her philosophy all along has been that those who hang out with dorks and wimps have dorky and wimpy things rub off on them. Then how come none of her ruggedness rubbed off on me?

When I look up, I see Von running after the float. She jumps on and takes the menehune head off Dennis Kawachi. Dennis holds his hands up in front of him. "I give up!" he screams. "No lick me." He isn't laughing anymore.

"Oh, please, Dennis. You laughing at my friend, you stupid Jap?" Von asks him.

"You half Jap yourself," Raleigh Rubianes says as he takes off his menehune head.

"I heard that!" Von yells. "You like me slap your head, hah, you tub of tar?"

"No, sorry, Von."

Babes runs alongside the float. Von pulls her aboard. "C'mon, Louie," Von says, holding out her hand to me. I get up off the road and start running toward her.

She takes the papier-mâché heads off Randall, who thanks her, and Yun Pui, who clings on to his head until Babes and Von pry his fingers away. Meanwhile, I jog alongside the float.

"Von," I call, "what you doing?"

She holds out her hand to me and clasps on tightly. For a while, my feet dangle until Babes reluctantly helps me up.

"No laughing at Emi-lou Kaya!" she yells as the float trudges up the road. "She bust her ass building this stupid float. Beat it," she tells the boys who recognize Von as one of the bulls of the school.

Everybody watches Dennis's skinny body in a twisted malo jump off the float and run toward the school, his Fruit of the Looms peeking out from under the loincloth.

Randall slumps down in the bed of the truck. "C'mon, Von, gimme a break. I half-naked," he says. "I wasn't laughing at Louie, right, Louie?"

I nod, full of power.

"I not wearing bibs, Von," Yun Pui says. "Pass me my shorts. You like them all see my grapes?"

Von stares at Raleigh, who heaves himself over the side and squeezes himself into the cab of the truck. Von laughs. She puts the *Fac.* menehune head on the top of the cab, the *7th* on Babes, the *8th* on her, and through the mouth hole, she says, "You the queen of the *ninth* grade, Louie." I put my head on.

She raises my hand in the air and shouts, "Unity!" Even Randall and Yun Pui start chanting with us. "No let go my hand, Louie," she says. "I no like you fall."

18.
Girls, Girls, Girls

I decide to wear long pants to hide the cuts on my knees. But the cuts on my face–I try to cover them with Band-Aids, but end up looking even stupider. Everybody starts calling me "Ouch." I don't care, because all I can think about is bad luck number three lurking around some dark corner.

By the time the first issue of *The Viking* comes out, I've written three feature articles as assistant to the features editor. I've also written three of Kyle's sports stories.

I'm not stupid. I know what was going on the couple of weeks before our first deadline. Kyle Kiyabu's body so close to mine in newswriting class, I could feel the hairs on my arm stand up and make static with his every time he gave me the information I needed to write his articles.

It's like only he and I existed in Period 6, the world closed to our bubble of arm touching and looking at his long, dark eyelashes and into his light brown eyes. And one day, our legs touched under the table. Kyle put his arm behind me on my chair and I wrote all three articles, plus my own articles, before the deadline.

At the end of class on all those days that he acted as though I were *his*, he'd say, "Eh, wait for me, Sissy." Then he pretended like he didn't know me anymore because he already got what he needed.

No matter what anybody says about how he's using me this and that, truthfully, I don't care. It feels good to have somebody like Kyle Kiyabu need me. I've secretly loved him for two years now, going on three. I have every newspaper article about him. I've been to every game. Whenever I see him, I ache in my bones for him to even notice me with the slightest glance.

I photocopied his picture from the yearbook, enlarged and framed it. I sleep with the musty old sleeping bag that he touched when we went camping at Puakō. And here I am, formerly fat, presently not-fat, but pill-popping, half-starving, jittery Emi-lou Kaya, writing *his* articles. He needs me. I feel honored.

Sterling and I walk to A-building bathroom after school, and one day before our last deadline, he says, "Hey, Louie. I know what you doing for Kyle."

I try to act innocent. "I don't know what you talking about."

"Louie, he telling all the girls," he says, "especially Sissy, and once he told her, the whole staff knew. Nobody like tell Hatayama 'cause we all no like get Kyle in trouble, but it ain't good for you, man. He telling everybody that you do anything for him. Get what I saying by *anything*, Louie?"

I fell like I'm falling from the sky. "No tell nobody,

okay, Sterling, please. No tell Von, especially." Sterling and I sit on the steps by A-building bathroom and he lights a cigarette.

"Louie, I can ask you something?" he says as he drags deeply. "I don't know how to ask this–" Then he looks at me for a long time. "You and Von–I mean, I ain't new to all that, and no bother me–you know, like Rae and Anita."

"They together, right? You think me and Von? I mean–" I've thought about Babes and Von being like Rae and Anita so many times. Anita always thinks about Rae, gives her aspirin, gets her towel, holds her wallet, and wears her jewelry. And Rae always watches out for Anita, if she's comfortable, if she needs money, if she's cold, opens and closes doors for her.

"My aunty Priscilla, you know, she one butchie," he says flinging his cigarette into a hibiscus bush. "I use to hang with all her friends, so no bother me, that's their trip. I used to tell my aunty, 'I no care if you like that.' And she used to tell me, 'No, it's 'cause you *do* care, that you want to know.' Something like that. So, I like know . . . no, I want to know. . . "

"What, I mean, why you have to know?" I ask him.

"'Cause maybe I–" He stumbles. "Maybe you . . . since the time I met you at Hāpuna Beach, I kinda, you know–"

"I know," I tell him. "I was fat."

"No, I not talking about that," he says. "I trying to tell you–" He turns toward the lockers. He head-jerks somebody with a small smile. "Never mind," he says.

"What?"

"Nothing," he says, "no worry. But you gotta tell me, what's up between you and Von?"

"She my best friend." I look toward the lower campus for Von to save me from his questions. "Me and Von, we both normal," I tell him.

"Normal?" Sterling laughs as he moves closer to me. "Look around this town," he says. "Look around this school, the softball league. Get plenty girls. This bathroom," he says, pointing toward the door, "girls, girls, girls—not real out in the open, but ain't no secret either, know what I mean? So what exactly is normal, right?"

I nod. "I closer to Von than anybody else in the whole world, even my own mother. But we not—" I want to tell him our whole history, how we were raised together, how she's outward for me and I'm inward for her, how we made a silent promise to protect each other with the blood. Something inside me knows I will tell him all of this one day. But not today.

Von and Babes round the corner at the bottom of the stairs. Sterling puts his hand on my knee and says, "I ain't saying nothing about our talk, promise."

I smile at Von. I believe him.

19.
Bad Luck Number Three

The day after the first issue of *The Viking* is released, Mrs. Hatayama calls me to her office. "Sit down, Emi-lou," she says. "I've been a teacher for years now and I want you to be honest with me, okay?" She looks me straight in the eye.

"Did you write Kyle Kiyabu's articles? Before you answer that—what triggered me was your writing style. Every writer has his own style. Your three articles and Kyle's three articles have the same sound and pace. Did you?"

I don't say anything. My lips start quivering. I don't care if I get an *F*. I don't want Kyle to think I squealed on him.

"No," I whisper. "I mean—"

"I won't say that you told. I already knew about it from what some of the editors shared with me—Kyle's been digging his own grave. I'll get *him* to admit it, don't worry. As for you, you're a lovely girl. Boys like Kyle are a dime a dozen—they're very nice to look at, and you probably won't understand this until you're older, but that kind of outer beauty fades very quickly. They'll use you all the time if you let them. Be careful."

I fix my eyes on a scribble of red pen on her blotter. A misshapen happy face. A series of blue swirls. "You going call my grandma?"

"No, I won't call home, this time," she says. "Your grandmother and I go back a long way in the department. But I will be dropping your grade for a lack of judgment."

Kyle sees me leave Mrs. Hatayama's office.

He swears under his breath. "Now I going flunk. How I going to play volleyball with one *F* this quarter?" he tells Sissy. "I bet you she told Hatayama."

Sterling walks over to me and whispers, "Sit down, no look at him, no say nothing."

"But I just—"

"So your grandma raise you and Von like sisters?" Sterling laughs nervously, but uses his huge body to shield Kyle's eyes from mine. "Nod, Louie, nod," he whispers. "And your grandma and Von love spooky movies but you too chicken, right?"

"Why you guys talking about me?"

"Kyle," Mrs. Hatayama says as she pokes her head from her office door. "May I see you for a minute, son?"

"Just nod and talk," Sterling says from between gritted teeth. Kyle gets up and glares at me as he passes. He steps into Mrs. Hatayama's office. The door closes.

Sterling exhales loudly. "We small-talk about this and that when he comes out, too."

"Thanks," I tell him, deflated and scared. I look

around the room. Nancy Nitta looks sympathetically at me. Jenni Takatani shrugs her shoulders in neutrality. Sissy shakes her head in disgust.

"What?" Sterling tells them all. "Get back to work."

"No worry. I use to this."

"What don't kill you—" he begins.

"Only make me stronger," I finish. He looks astonished. "My grandma always tell me that."

"Mine, too," he says.

Kyle steps out of the office and mouths terrible swear words at me, his back to the teacher.

"So next time your grandma and Von rent spooky movies," Sterling says, grabbing my full attention away from Kyle's stream of ugly words, "invite me, okay."

I nod.

A piece of sky falls on me. Bad luck number three. Sick in my gut, I want to eat something, plenty of warm food. I feel weightless. I feel fat. I put my head on the desk. I don't want anybody to see my good-for-nothing face. And all I can think about is food.

20.

Big Island Women's Softball League Champs

Carvalho Park, when illuminated at night, looks neon green. I like the sound of the lights going on, that surge of big electricity, the lights humming above my head.

The Hilo Astros win a close game against the Kona Gold to take the Big Island Women's Softball League Champs. Even though Coach Kaaina doesn't play me, not one minute, I don't mind. At least she let me suit up for all the games. It gives me a shred of dignity.

The league holds a big awards ceremony after the championship game. The sports writer from the *Hilo Tribune Herald*, Reggie Okamura, and the mayor of the Big Island county, Geofrey Oshiro, are on hand to pass out the trophies.

"We'd like to announce the All-Island First Team Picks before we hand out the championship trophy to the Hilo Astros," Reggie Okamura says into the public address system.

"In left field, All-Star honors go to Kathy Cachola of the Waiākea Uka Alapas. Center field, Claire Shimizu from the Kona Gold. Right field, Francine Souza, from the Honoka'a Maile Women."

The whole crowd cheers because the individual trophies are a big thing in the league. These awards honor the best on the whole island.

"At catcher, Kennie Sakamoto from Kona Gold. First base, Rae Kalani of the Hilo Astros. Second base, Gina Mahina of the Kaūmana Krew. Shortstop, Lynden Shigezawa from the Waiākea Uka Alapas. And at third base, our youngest awardee in the history of the league and a relative newcomer in her first appearance in the Women's Softball League, Yvonne Vierra, Hilo Astros."

I can't believe my ears. I turn to Von, but she turns to Babes and they hug for a long time. Von runs up to the platform real macho-style and waves at me.

Reggie Okamura announces the pitching awards. A hush comes over the whole Carvalho Park. "The award for Outstanding Pitcher goes to Merla Ah Chong of the Hilo Astros. Let's give the women a big hand."

When I look at Von up there on the platform, it's like that's me, too. The whole team comes back to the bench and everyone's jumping and high-fiving and hugging. Von comes back—then she, Babes, and I all hug together. I don't want to include Babes in what is Von's and mine, but Von holds her close.

"Ho, my daughter, Yvonne, come here," Uncle Charlie says as he walks toward Von, squatting with arms outspread like an orangutan. He low-fives and high-fives Von and bear-hugs her. He gives her three strands of puakenikeni. This is the first time Uncle doesn't say very much. He keeps his arm around Von and basks in her glory.

"Charlie, my dear," Aunty Etsuko says, "Yvonne has other fans, you know. Squeeze your butt out, now." She and Grandma each give Von a maile lei.

This is what I wanted for Von. Bedecked in lei all the way to her eyes, I know she's on her way to a four-year scholarship. It was a hard season for me. Every day, my reasons for being on the team changed. I worked hard. I played halfheartedly. I was berated daily. I choked. Then I dug deeper into myself to stay on the team. I even got to play a couple of times. I got better. I got worse. Some days, I was playing for Von. Then I was playing for me. And somewhere around the playoffs, I was just doing it. But who am I kidding? By the end of the season, I just I wanted to keep Babes away from Von.

When I turn, I see my grandma. "Here, Emi-lou," she says. "You hung in there and that's what matter to me. Was me, I give up long time ago, but not you. You junk ball player, but you get character. Inside here," she says, pointing to my chest, "you tough. Next season, you be that much better." She gives me a nice maile lei.

"That's so true. You'll get better and better. And you're the best sister Yvonne could ever have," Aunty Ets says as she gives me a pakalana lei. It almost sounds like she *knows* what I was up to sitting all those long, hot games at the end of the bench, taking laps for being clumsy, recording pages of stats, and filling all the water bottles, too.

I have two lei, which are plenty for me. All the other girls wear lei to their eyebrows. The Hilo Astros always take a team picture bedecked in flowers. That's their tradition. And this year, the photographer from the newspaper's here.

Somebody taps my shoulder. "My grandma can be hell on wheels, you know it, Louie." Sterling stands there with Kyle behind him.

Kyle smirks. He's still mad about newswriting class. Kyle walks away and I watch as he slinks through the crowd.

"Here, Louie, come here," Sterling says as he puts the nicest maunaloa lei on me. "I made this myself. Hard, you know, make this lei."

"I know, take days just to gather all the flowers."

"No mind Kyle," he says. "Just like all his big brothers and druggie uncles. All boneheads." Sterling kisses my cheek and hugs me, brother-style. "Go, they taking the team picture."

All the girls line up in front of the winning dugout. Even Aunty Vicky has lei up to her nose. Babes and Von stand with each other.

Von yells, "C'mon, Louie." The cameraman's saying one, two—and Von yells, "Wait, wait. Ho, hold it." All the girls moan and groan.

She starts to put her lei on me. Now I'm to my chin and she's up to her mouth. Choochie gives me one. Then Anita runs over to Rae and takes two lei from her to give to me with a light kiss.

"You part of this, too, Louie," Von says.

"I'd say," Anita adds.

"Smile, girlfriend," Rudy calls, "you in the spotlight."

"Deep, Louie-Louie, deeper than the deep blue sea."

We both laugh as the camera flashes.

21.
Hilo High Viking Men

Boys' volleyball tryouts start. Huggie and Erma Kaaina coach the Hilo High Viking Men team. Lucky for Hilo, Sterling transferred from Pāhoa High, because he's a hustler and a smart six-feet-four setter– an Erma Kaaina-designed, strategic position for her NCAA-bound grandson.

"Eh, Von," Babes says one day at A-building bathroom, "like take stats with me and Viva for the boys? Aunty Erma like her girls to help out, 'cause the boys come out for us when softball season."

Her girls. I know that term of affection doesn't include me.

"Shoots," Von says, "but where I go–"

And the girls finish for her, "Louie-Louie go, too."

"So what, Von, you guys *going* or what?" Babes asks and they look at each other for a long time, their eyes saying something heartfelt and secretive. "Well, tell your shadow be at the gym by three o'clock every day after school."

"You better not wise off, Kris," I tell her as Von nudges me hard, "right, Von? Tell her."

"No wise off at Louie," Von says in a sarcastic, robotic monotone. "Babes, you hear me?" Babes laughs.

By the time we come to take stats, Huggie and Coach Kaaina have already made the cuts. They've kept twelve players. Huggie calls everybody to the bench.

"We one man short for the first couple games." The whole team falls silent. "I expect you boys to pick up the slack and hang in there till we clear our player with the school administration. I already in negotiations with the counselors and the teacher involved, so until we iron things out, you guys hang tight."

Coach Kaaina butts in. "What Huggie saying in plain English is that Kyle didn't make the two-point-oh to play because of an *F* in one of his classes, a stinking elective at that." She shoots her eyes right at me. "But since Sterling in that class, he helping Kyle from now on. But we all pray for Kyle and Huggie, so we can clear his name." She stares me down and then snubs me.

I don't get it. I mean, Kyle was wrong and now the whole team's going to pray for him? And what makes me angrier is how he acts so innocent.

Huggie walks over to Viva, Von, Babes, and me. "You girls be responsible for the bags and water bottles," he says, "two of you always on stats, and I want the job to rotate. Fold the boys' warm-up suits on the back of their chair—and lastly, girls, look gorgeous at every game. Don't come to games dressed like slobs. Wear the school colors. It's part of your job. Smile and no grumble, you hear me?"

After practice, I see Sterling talking to Von and Babes by her truck. When I approach them, he wipes his sweat on my arm and Von says, "Oh, that's gross, man, Sterling." He laughs and wipes my arm with his towel.

"So, I call you tonight, Von," Sterling says. "Tonight after nine. Spark you laters, ladies."

Kyle gets in the front with Babes because he might catch a cold in the back. Von and I climb in the back. "What's that all about?" I ask Von. "How come Sterling calling you tonight? You get something *going* with him, Von?" I tease.

"No tell nobody, okay, Louie? What am I saying? Of course, you not going tell nobody."

"He asked you to *go* with him? Omigod, Von, say yes," I tell her. The minute I say this, I know it sounds fake. But I still want her to think that I think she's normal and to discourage her from being a lez.

She puts her arm around my neck and headlocks me. "Nah, me and Sterling close. I help him, he help me. Viva been coming on strong and yesterday after practice, she asked him to *go* with her. He like me let her down easy."

"Nah? For real, Von? What's his problem? Viva cute, what you think, Von?" After I ask, I regret asking that of Von.

"She all right." We pull into my driveway and I jump out.

"Call me after then, Von." And she gives me a low shaka which means yes.

"How long you guys was talking?"

"One hour half till my dad said get off now before I boff your head."

"One hour half? What Sterling said?"

"Nah, nothing much."

"How can be nothing much if you talk that long? What he said about Viva?"

"Nah, nothing."

"Von, why you holding out on me?"

"Nah, nothing."

"Okay, Von, whatevers."

"Ho, no need get mad, Louie. Ask Sterling yourself. He said he going with us trick-or-treat this weekend. You get that whole damn trick-or-treat for UNICEF can to fill for Rudy Rudman, right?"

"Yeah, like Sterling going tell me his love problems."

"Why, you guys close, no act, Louie."

"Not like how you close to him, Von."

"No worry, ask him, he tell you. After we do your trick-or-treat for UNICEF thing, Sterling said to come to the high school Halloween Dance. So, Louie-Louie . . . we cannot wear costumes this year to trick-or-treat for UNICEF. Aw shucks, no, Louie?"

She says this like I'm the one who wants to dress up for Halloween. She's the one who always wants to be a football player with all the pads and black eye stuff every year.

"Okay, whatevers, Von."

"And he said make sure next time me and your grandma watch spook movies to invite him."

"Yeah, he told me that, too."

"See, Louie. He close with you."

"Right." If Von only knew he'd asked me about *us*, she'd flip out. "Bye."

"Bye, Louie-Louie."

I hang up the phone. I look at Von standing next to me in that Hilo Astros picture. I smell the maunaloa lei from Sterling drying perfectly over my bureau mirror. I stare at my photocopied picture of Kyle. I turn off my bedroom light.

22.

Trick-or-treat
for UNICEF

Only the ultradedicated members of the student council agree to trick-or-treat for UNICEF this year. And some of them, I know, keep the money they collect.

But Rudy Rudman says on Halloween day at the UNICEF drive meeting, "Girlfriends and assorted boyfriends, let's be honest and make more money than they ever seen at this school 'cause that's the kind of prez I am—all-out and all-the-way, or no way. So turn in all your money, honey, and no take out nothing for your own personal charities. Two snaps around the heart for honesty."

"So what you saying, Rudy?" Judith Wong asks. "That we was ripping off in the past?"

"Oh please, girlfriend. Please no be acting like this the first time you heard of this. Even certain ex-friends of yours truly been known to benefit from UNICEF stash cash, but no names." He pauses. "Sanford Hata and Benjamin Perez," he whispers.

"The list of participants, Miss Louie. Thank you, dahling. Now, tell them what you did as my personal presidential aide."

"I took a soup can same size as the UNICEF can and filled um up with a variety of coins. Then I counted um all up."

"So?" Judith says.

"So?" Rudy barks. "So we know approximately how much dough you all be coughing up tomorrow."

That night, Babes picks me up last. Sterling jumps out from the front. "Go in the back, keep Sterling company," Von says, leaning out the window. "Where you like go, Louie? You like go guys' house we know or just around rich places like Reeds Island or what?"

"Guys' house we don't know 'cause I know you guys going tease me and make me tell 'Trick-or-treat for UNICEF' all the time," I tell Von.

"I go with you," Sterling says. "We go house we know, Babes. Go down Keaukaha, house lots, and Waiākea Uka. I help you guys fill this whole can."

"What you mean, you guys? This Louie's thing, man," Von says. She and Babes laugh like I'm the silliest, uncoolest turd for doing things like this for Rudy's causes.

"Here's my contribution to the can." Sterling's coins jangle at the bottom. This marks the first time anybody helped me fill my UNICEF can. Von always goes along only for the Halloween candy. When he gives the can back to me, he doesn't move his hand, so my hand touches his.

We trick-or-treat for UNICEF all over town. The

can's almost full. The night air rushes past us as we climb the last street to Coach Kaaina's house deep in the Pana'ewa forest.

Babes takes off her jacket and drapes it over Von's shoulders. They walk ahead of us. In the streetlight, they look like a real couple taking a child out to fill a plastic jack-o'-lantern with candies. I want to tear the jacket off of Von.

"You cold, Louie?" I don't say yes, I don't say no, but before I know it, Sterling's warm volleyball jacket hangs on me. We stand on Coach Kaaina's porch.

"I get this one." Sterling yells, "Trick-or-treat for UGLY-CEF!"

Coach Kaaina comes out and the screen door slams behind her. "Ugly-cef? You guys the ugly ones." And then she tells the oldest joke around. "Take off your mask so I can see who you are." Everybody laughs like that's the first time they heard that joke because she told it. "Oohhh, is that you, my sweetheart grandson?" she says planting a wet one on Sterling's lips. "Howzit, Babes, Von." She greets them both with kisses and then shields her eyes as if to see better in the dark. "Is that Emi-lou? Oh, whateva." I wave meekly at her. She can see that it's me.

"Now, Sterling, sweetie, you come home early tonight. Right after the dance. No Wailoa, no nothing, you hear me?" She turns around sharply and looks at me on the bottom of her steps.

She sees me in Sterling's jacket, narrows her eyes, and grits her teeth. She doesn't say anything, then she drops some nickels in my can.

Nobody's good enough for my NCAA-bound grandson, her eyes seem to say. Besides, I hate typical, middle-class Japs like you.

"I love you, sweetie," she says as she smacks another one on Sterling's lips.

23.

The Halloween
Dance

We get to the ticket booth at the gym. Sterling and Babes show their high school IDs. Then Sterling whispers something to Sissy Miyamoto, who's the ticket girl, takes out his wallet, and pays for Von and me. "Walk in close by my side. Babes, shield them," he says.

"You saying I fat?" she tells him.

"No, I saying you make a good shield. They not suppose to be here, only high school." We sneak in and right away, Sterling says, "Go over there."

I sit in the corner by a folded trampoline with Sterling next to me. Babes presses her back against the dusty wall and Von sits next to her. Babes leans into Von's hair and whispers something to Von, who gives a breathy laugh.

"I no mean to be rude, you guys. I promise, Louie"– and Sterling looks at me like he means this–"but I supposed to meet Kyle and Baron them. I told them I be here. I didn't think I had to sit in this dark corner to baby-sit. Nah, Von, just kidding. I come right back."

Baby-sit? Although he's joking, for some reason it

makes me uncomfortable. Like a private joke between Sterling and Von. His leaving interrupts Babes and Von for a brief moment. But Von continues to exclude me. I wonder if Sterling's attention toward me has something to do with their conversation the other night. Maybe he's supposed to keep me distracted.

It's so dark here. Von seems totally unaware of me. She briefly leans her head on Babes's shoulder. The gym begins to feel very humid and just as I take off Sterling's jacket to hit Von over the head with it, the boys all come back. Viva follows them.

She looks at me and asks Von, "Whose volleyball jacket Louie wearing?" Viva looks at all the boys. One by one, they hold up their hands like, "Not me, not me."

"Yours, Sterling?"

"I had it 'cause we went trick-or-treat for UNICEF and got cold—" I don't even finish before the whole group of boys, Kyle the loudest, yells, "Trick-or-treat for UNICEF?" like that was the stupidest, babiest thing to do.

Everybody's laughing so hard that Viva's forced to laugh, too. I give Sterling back his jacket. He folds it and puts it on my lap. Viva stares at me, then at Von, and Von kicks me in the leg. I know Viva likes Sterling.

A slow song comes on. Viva grabs Sterling's hand and pulls him up on the dance floor. I look at Kyle to say with my eyes, "Dance with me," but he's gone. Across the crowded floor, I see him holding hands with Sissy Miyamoto, and they clamp their bodies together right next to Sterling and Viva.

Von scoots toward me. "Kyle is such a dog, Louie. Stop even wishing for that hound to—"

"You don't know what I thinking, so don't even try it," I tell her. "You no like even sit next to me."

"Whatevers," Von says, giving me a shove from behind.

Babes takes out a fifth of Bacardi from her backpack and she and Von drink from the bottle. Kyle comes off the floor. He doesn't even walk Sissy back to her popular friends.

"Eh, Babes," he says, "where my bottle? Cannot be sharing germs with you kiddies, right?"

Babes opens her backpack. "Drinks, my friends," she says, "is on my house."

Sterling sits next to me. "Pass me my jacket, Louie." He wraps a small bottle in its sleeve. Viva sits by Sterling with her legs crossed so that her leg rests on his leg. He moves a little bit closer to me and leans back with his hand behind me.

I don't know why he doesn't like Viva. She's really pretty with a cutesy voice, the super-sweet Miss Teen USA, good-girlfriend type. She's in the same grade with him. But Sterling's not even looking at Viva; he just stares at the dance floor. "You like, Louie?" he says as he hands me the bottle. I shake my head no. "You like?" he asks Viva. She takes the bottle and tanks a big one so that some rum dribbles down her lip. She licks her lip right in front Sterling.

He turns to me. "Like dance?"

We dance for about five songs and we're having a lot of fun. The skinny part of me wants to like Sterling. The fat part of me inside keeps reminding me: Who you kidding, chubs? He doesn't like you, fatso. He's only your friend, dork. You're making a fool of yourself, Fat Albert. It's all in your mind, you white whale. Better if you keep on dreaming about Kyle. That's safer, stupid. You want them to all laugh at you when you fall on your face over Sterling?

A slow song comes on. Viva stands on the side with her hands on her hips.

"You *going* with Viva, Sterling?" I ask. "Your girlfriend's pissed."

"Viva acting all nuts, Louie. Oh, wow, I all sweaty. Never mind, yeah, Louie? I just wipe my arm on her." He laughs with me for a moment and walks off toward Viva.

Viva puts her face on his chest and rubs his back. Sterling looks at me and smiles goofy. Then he pretends to wipe his sweaty arm all over her back.

Von's sitting so close to Babes. Everybody here must know what's going on. Who does Von think she's kidding? They're whispering and giggling and touching each other too much.

I can't believe it.

Von doesn't even see me. Whose house is she going to sleep over tonight? Not Babes. Von puts her fingers in Babe's hair. She brushes it out of her face just as she'd done so many times for me. I want to scream but I'm stunned.

Kyle sees me staring numbly and says, "We go dance, Emi-lou." He leads me far away from Sterling.

"No go by the teachers 'cause Von and me not suppose to be here," I tell him.

He doesn't like you, the fat Emi-lou reminds me, as I pull myself out of the trance. He takes me away from Sissy and her friends so that they cannot see him either.

"You look nice," he tells me, his eyes red, small, and

unfocused. He's feeling no pain. He starts rubbing my back. I try to get away; he's being too rough. "You can help me, Emi-lou? If you don't, I cannot play volleyball and I going mess up my chance for scholarship. It's all up to you, whether I get chance to play NCAA or not. You get my very life in your hands." He's talking like he's real deep.

Right when he says that, he puts my face in his hands and kisses me, then his mouth slides over my neck. My whole body tingles with nausea and pleasure; my feet don't feel like they're on the floor. Kyle says, "I guess that's a yes, right, Emi-lou?"

I guess it is. It's hard not to believe that he really does like me, kissing me like that in front of half of the high school.

When the song ends, he walks away from me toward Sissy and her friends. I take the long walk back to the dark corner. "Hey, Louie," Sterling says, "where you was?"

Viva's wearing his jacket. Sterling leans over and whispers to me, "We better do something about Von. She kind of feeling it. She going get in trouble or what?"

"She sleeping over at my house tonight."

"You all right, Louie?" he asks. I nod quickly when I hear Kyle's voice approaching. "We better get her out of the gym," Sterling tells me.

The lights begin spinning, the music slows, then the DJ says, "Last dance, the very, very last dance. I want you to move the one you love to the dance floor for some Atlantic Starr."

Sterling looks at me. Even though he said we'd better leave, he takes my hand in his. "C'mon, Louie, you and me. We didn't dance one slow one yet." He leads me to the middle of the floor and puts his arms around my waist. I can hardly reach his shoulders. He has to sort of bend down. He starts pulling me closer until I see Von and Babes in the dark corner.

"Look, Sterling," I tell him.

"What?"

"Von and Babes, they drunk, they getting all–"

Sterling takes my hand and walks over to them. He signals that we all have to leave before the lights in the gym go on. The four of us hurry out of there. Viva follows and Kyle leaves Sissy midsentence because Babes is his ride home.

We cross the street and everybody continues partying in the parking lot. The lights from the gym go off and all the teachers pull out of the school.

Kyle walks up to Sterling and says, "Slow dancing with my *A* in newswriting and English and social studies, eh, Sterling?"

"What? Eh, Kyle, back off. You drunk," he says as he shoves him off with both hands. "No use her."

Kyle says, "No, you back off." He pushes Sterling. "You like go states or what, hah? I know what I doing. *You* back off. I need the grades." Levi and Spencer pull them apart.

"Bonehead," Sterling tells him. "Your whole family, boneheads."

"My whole family? My big brothers, my uncles, my cousins, they go jail for me for less than that. Lip-off, punk, they kick your ass. Right, Cuz?" Babes steps up and leads Kyle away.

Even though I lied to myself for about five minutes that Kyle liked me, it still hurts to hear him talk like that.

And Sterling—if he likes me, then why slow dance with Viva? So what if she got mad? Would she make a better girlfriend in the eyes of the boys? Some kind of macho peer pressure? I just don't get it.

I feel so ashamed, until Viva says, "What the hell you guys fighting about, man? Let's go Wailoa. Bust out the buds, boys." Her flippant words lighten up the whole situation.

"Louie," Von says as she leans her heavy arm across my shoulders. I move her out of the way and climb in the front seat of Babes's truck. Von gets angry. She shoves her shoulder right into mine. "Take us home, Babes," I say. "My grandma waiting to take the breath test on us."

"Oh, no, Louie, I forgot," Von says.

"See you, Von. Why you had to drink?"

"I only took few sips," she tells me.

"Come sleep over my house, Von," Babes says quickly. "Nobody give a rip what time I come home. We can sleep downstairs in the playroom."

I think fast. "No. I mean, Von cannot. You better listen to me, Yvonne," I tell her. "Your father going get mad if you not at my house tomorrow morning when he call to check on you. You just wait outside by the car till I take the breath test. After my grandma go sleep, I let you in the house."

"Get out of my face, Louie," she says to me.

"My name is Emi-lou," I tell her.

Babes starts snickering. "Lovers' quarrel?" she asks Von.

"Oh, please," Von sneers. "Emi-lou here is just mad 'cause your cuz danced with Sissy all night."

"You like Kyle, Louie?" Babes guffaws. "Wait till I tell him this one. Nah, here's my advice: Get in the back of the line, girlfriend."

I feel sick. How could Von do this to me? It's over. It's all over. I feel so embarrassed. "I not your girlfriend," I tell Babes. "You better not say nothing. Von drunk. She like Kyle, not me."

"You talking bubbles, Louie," Von says as she elbows me hard in the ribs. "Next time I sleep over your house, Babes. Louie get curfew tonight. I have to go her house."

I look at Babes. She doesn't look at me. She knows I've won. And then she glances at me: *This time.*

When we get to my house, I turn around and see Kyle, Levi, Sterling, and Viva in the back of the truck. Kyle jumps out to ride up front with Babes. "Scram," he says to me, blowing me a sarcastic kiss.

Viva's wearing Sterling's jacket and her head's resting on his shoulder. He gives me the goofy smile and says softly, "Hey, Louie-Louie, trick-or-treat for UNICEF, you get your can?" I shake it softly. "I call you up tomorrow to check on Von." Viva winds her arm around his and snuggles into his body. "And you, Lou. I calling to check on you."

They pull slowly out of my grandma's driveway, into the orange streetlights, and disappear down the road.

24.
Mind Games

Almost every weekend, the boys' volleyball team plays an out-of-town game. Huggie seems pleased with *his* girls, because we don't need to be told what to do. Von organizes us incredibly well.

"Viva, take stats with Louie," she says, "Babes, get the water bottles. I get the bags and the warm-ups. Louie, make sure Huggie get ice water and Coach Kaaina her Coke. The color for the Honoka'a game is navy blue."

She gets ready for the games at my house so she can French-braid or crimp my hair. And she picks out an outfit for me. Usually, Viva and I wear dresses, nothing fancy, but nice, with panty hose and sandals. Von and Babes wear Gap clothes. And Von gels her hair.

My grandma says right before we leave, "How many Spam musubi you like me make for the boys? Yvonne, you got enough soda for the Honoka'a game tonight? Where the cooler? How many Spam musubi, Emi-lou? Yvonne? Somebody better answer me before you find yourself making your own food."

Von had asked Grandma and Aunty Etsuko to be team-moms, then she organized the entire crew of team-mothers for the potlucks after the games.

Huggie and Coach Kaaina pick up Von and me in the van. Babes, Sterling, and Viva are already there. My grandma comes out of the house with a soda box full of Saran-wrapped musubi. "Howzit, everybody," she says peering into the van. "Sterling, you ready to smash Honoka'a?"

"Oh, yes," he answers, "and thanks for the food, Mrs. Kaya, and for the drummettes and sushi you made for the last game."

"You get good memory for food, eh, Sterling?" Grandma laughs.

"Yeah, I hinting for dinner invitation," he says to her. "I know how to make baked crab salad."

"Real crab?" Grandma asks.

"Yup," he says. "And I love spooky movies. I like come next time with Von."

"Any time. You know where I live."

"You mark my words," Coach Kaaina tells Grandma, "you going live to regret inviting this chowhound to dinner. Just look at him, Leatrice. He going on six-five. I tell you, he can eat. But lucky thing he take after me in the looks category and not this one," she says pointing her thumb at Huggie.

"You win tonight," Grandma says, "and I soak the kal-bi and stuff the eggplant before you get home."

"And I rent all the Halloween movies."

"I hate that kine movies," I grumble.

"You can sit by me," Sterling says. "I cover your ears and Von get your eyes."

"Promise?" I ask.

He nods and smiles.

I kind of like Sterling, but really, this all makes me so uncomfortable. It's way more complicated than liking somebody from afar. I'm so used to being the only one in love. But I have to admit, this feels good in a queasy-tingly sort of way.

"Louie," Von calls, "try help me." She lifts the heavy cooler from the garage and Sterling gets out to help her. "We be home late tonight, Lea," Huggie says. "Looks like we might go three games the way the Dragons been playing."

"Yeah, no worry. You girls have jackets? Sheez, these two like chicken without a head. Vicky," she yells toward the house, "bring the kids couple jackets."

"Ho, boy," Von groans, "kids?" I get in fast and sit next to Babes. Von's forced to sit next to me–she gets even more mad. Then Von gives Sterling a look like, see-what-I-mean-about-Louie-always-squeezing-her-butt-in. Sterling sits behind us next to Viva.

He puts his hands on my shoulders, his head between us and says, "Don't forget your jacket, kids." Viva giggles.

"Don't get comfortable," Coach Kaaina announces. "We riding on the bus 'cause us and the athletic direc-tor, Mr. Teixeira, chaperoning the boys." Everybody complains. "Oh, be quiet," she says. "And 'cause we ranked high in the states this year, Mr. Teixeira send-ing one pep bus with cheerleaders for the rest of our out-of-town games. How you like that?"

"Nah?" Sterling says. "We rate then, yeah, Gramma?

Ho, would be bad if we took states. Kyle gotta keep up his grades, that's the only thing. Then, look out, Punahou, we getting your crown at states."

Huggie breaks in, "Eh, no worry about Kyle. He been buckling down. He wen' raise his grades from *F* to *C* already in newswriting. His English grades, too. Now he tell me his social studies coming next, how you like that? We so proud of him." I hope they don't think their prayers have been helping Kyle's grade.

I didn't tell Sterling or Von that I was still writing Kyles articles. I wrote them in a really simpleminded way. I used that same style and wrote some of his English papers. He's gotten *B*s ever since. Kyle thinks that touching his leg to mine and smiling with those dimples is making me do his work. But the thrills aren't that major anymore. I just don't want him to be mad at me. And I don't want him to be mad at Sterling.

Huggie pulls into the parking lot next to the gym. A few players arrive and start unloading their gear. Sterling catches me behind the van where Von and I are loading the cooler onto the bus. "Here, give me your side, Louie."

"No, Huggie said we girls have to do our own job," Von says. But Sterling takes it anyway. He leans over and whispers something to Von. "Yeah, I know. No worry, brah, I got it all under control," she says to Sterling.

"What? What you get under control?" I ask.

"Never mind." Von acts as though she's irritated with me. "Go load the ball bags, Louie."

"What you guys talking about, Sterling?"

He shrugs his shoulders and ducks behind the bus.

All these mind games. Sometimes I feel really close to Sterling. But I know he's close to Von, too. He calls her up a lot. Are they talking about me? Von would say something. Sometimes it feels like they're plotting, then I think I'm being paranoid.

Viva's wearing the tightest turquoise Lycra dress with matching turquoise pumps. Her hair's French-braided with baby's breath and Maui roses. She's wearing a lot of makeup with glossy lipstick. She's hanging close to Sterling so she can sit with him on the bus. After we finish loading all the gear, coolers, and food, Von yells, "Eh, Viva, try come."

"What for?" Viva yells back.

"'Cause you didn't help us load nothing. Go get the lineup from Coach Huggie, right now. He like you trade list with Honoka'a as soon as we get to the gym."

"Tell Louie. She taking stats tonight, too."

"No, you taking stats. Louie been doing everything while you been standing around looking pretty."

"You always backing her up, Von. Not fair. I telling Aunty Erma." Viva comes stomping over in her high heels and says, "Sterling, wait for me, okay?"

Sterling grabs my arm and pulls me in the bus. Babes motions, "Over here, over here." Sterling sits in the seat in front of Babes. He pushes me in toward the window. Pretty soon, Von comes in the bus and sits by Babes.

"Hi, babe," Babes says to her.

Viva walks in behind Von. She throws herself onto the seat in front of Sterling and me. "So how come you didn't save a seat for me, hah, Sterling?" She whirls her body around and crosses her arms. "Kyle, Kyle, I saved this seat for you." Viva turns around and smiles at me.

They all think I don't know what's going on. I know Von wanted to distract Viva when she gave her all of those extra duties outside of the bus. I know Viva wants to make me jealous by asking Kyle to sit by her. I know why I'm sitting *in front* of Von and Babes, too. That must've been part of the deal. So I can't see. So I can't interfere. So I'm not the third wheel. And does Sterling really want to sit with me or is that just a part of this game?

What does it matter? I'm losing Von so fast. I never know what's coming next, how I need to think, what I have to do. Sterling's in on it all the time. And Babes acts more and more cocky to me lately. What scares me is that when Babe wises off, Von doesn't do or say anything like she did before.

The bus rolls across the bridge over the Wailuku River. Outside, the wind feels dark and cool. Viva starts giggling as Kyle leans in toward her hair. She puts her hand on his leg and whispers something to him. Then she kisses his ear.

"That's it," Sterling says, and he takes my hand and starts moving to the back of the bus.

"Eh, whassup, Sterling?" Von whispers.

"You sit behind that tuna," he says. Viva turns around and snubs him.

When we settle into the back seat, Sterling puts his arm over my leg. He rests on my shoulder. "That's why I no like Viva," he tells me.

He straightens up and leans close to me. "But you, Louie, you–" He struggles for a moment. "Never mind, I tell you later."

"Would kinda help if you told me now," I stutter. His body so close to mine makes my upper lip and palms sweaty.

"I just no like you be seeing tunas in action, know what I mean?" he says.

I feel my body stiffen. "Everybody saying that since I, you know, since Von help me lose, you know–" I feel so uncomfortable talking about my body. "That I look like her."

"You ain't like Viva," he says.

I look at Sterling's dark skin, his strong hands. This is nothing like what I felt for Kyle. This is a gnawing knot and a flighty tingle jumbled together in the pit of my belly. I look at Sterling's handsome face. I must be the fat girl who's still making all of this up. No, this is some plan he devised with Von and Babes. He looks at me with soft eyes. I can't pretend anymore.

He takes off his jacket and covers me with it. We both fall asleep–but I only pretend to be asleep. I don't know if this is me in this body. This boy's body next to mine, his warm hand resting between my thighs.

25.
V-a-B

A-building bathroom, that's what the rest of the school calls Jap Bathroom. Nobody says anything bad about the bathroom in the open. It's where all the girls hang out. I don't go in there at recess time or any time. I use the bathroom in the library.

The high school is full of corners established generations ago. Football Corner, Pirates, A-V Room, Wreckers, Band, Pāpaʻikou Corner, Keaukaha Corner, the Patio, Senior Corner, and Jap Bathroom.

The girls smoke cigarettes and dope in there. The teachers do their best for the most part. But some security guards act like campus buddies, so nobody gets busted. Lots of girls from Jap Bathroom walk around stoned the whole day.

The stalls get marked, too. Not with graffiti like in other bathrooms at our school with blown-up toilets and broken sinks—the stalls in A-bathroom get marked for the girls. The couples who *go* together hang out there. They tape black velvet posters on the inside of their stalls, Town & Country stickers, and shiny stick-on letters.

After the Honoka'a game, Von and Babes ride back into town on the long backseat with Sterling and me. Von sits real close to Babes. On Monday, they go to school and mark their stall in A-bathroom.

V-a-B. Von and Babes in shiny, stick-on letters. I know this is not the same as V-a-L with a Sharpie marker on a restroom bench at JCPenney. I want to scream, *She's my best friend. Give her back to me.*

They're not friends. They're more than friends. I just want it the way we used to be, V-a-L.

They put up posters and surf stickers all over the stall in the back of the smoky bathroom. And when the bell rings, they go inside and lock the door.

I know I've lost Von. Sterling hangs out with me on the steps. He never acts like Von forced him to sit with me, but everybody seems to be looking and wondering why. Why is Sterling Jardine hanging out with the dorky Jap nobody? All the other volleyball boys have a cheerleader and majorette, one on each arm. Sterling seems so natural and relaxed. I feel like a fat sausage in a hot frying pan. Why is he with *her?* they all say with their glances and stares. I'm not even sure I am with him in the way they mean.

Von and I walk up together to the high school campus during recess, and she heads directly toward the bathroom.

"What you do in there anyway?" I ask her bluntly.

"We . . . we talk," she mutters.

"Right," I tell her. "You and me talk. We no need be

in close quarters to do that. When was the last time we talked in the same toilet stall, hah, Yvonne? Preschool?"

"Louie, I want you to . . . " she starts. "Oh, never mind."

"Want me to what? Join you in there? Okay. When?"

"Shut up," Von says. "I trying to make you understand—"

"Understand what?" I hiss at her. "That a fat pig like Babes is more—is your—"

"You use to be fat, too, Louie," Von says.

"This not about fat!" I yell at Von. Sterling jumps off of the railing. He smiles and ruffles Von's hair. "Get away from us," I tell him.

Von shoves me hard. "I listen to every damn detail of your stupid life," she tells me. "I trying to tell you that—"

"That what?" I say, shoving her back.

"That you better shape up and get your head out of your—" Babes walks toward Von. "You some *friend*, Louie, you know that?"

"You got me now, Von," Babes says staring me down.

"I got you in *me*, Von," I tell her.

"Shove this in you, Louie," she says flipping the bird in my face. "You got nothing in you."

26.
My Own Business

The only reason I knew what the stall looked like was because I came up to A-building bathroom while I had newswriting. I was shocked. The only time I'd been in there at recess was to get something for Von. It was then that I saw the occupied stalls. One pair of feet faced out. The other one faced in. And from behind the locked doors, I knew what they were doing.

Now I try to imagine Von doing that. I cannot even begin to picture it. Sterling sits on the concrete wall by A-building bathroom and tells me, "Actually, Louie, to me, and this is only my opinion—mind your own business."

"Von is my business," I tell him. "You mind your own business."

"I am minding my own business," he says smiling at me. I imagine he's referring to us but even that's very unclear. If Von weren't so mad at me, we would talk about this into the wee hours of morning. With her advice, I would know exactly what to do and how to act.

But lately, I feel like I can't talk to Von anymore. There's something deeper than the deep blue sea between us, and we both know what it is, but we can't name it.

"We? Me?" I stammer.

"You," he says. "Relax. You choking."

"Again," I tell him. "I always do that."

"Listen, what Von do, she going do," he says. "You cannot stop her. If you love her like you say, then let her go. You want her to hate you?"

He pulls me toward him.

"Baby-sitting for Von?" Kyle whispers to Sterling as he passes us with Sissy Miyamoto.

"Baby-sitting?" I ask, stepping back from Sterling.

"Let it go, Louie," he says. "I mean, screw him. You and me can hang out outside here if we like, right? Free country."

I shrug my shoulders.

Sterling looks toward the bathroom door. "Look at things like this," he says, "when recess is over, you get Von to yourself again. When you go home, she all yours. But you better face it—they more than you think. And you gotta learn to share."

"I hate Babes."

"She ain't that bad, Louie. She help me through some pretty rough times. I can see what Von see in her—"

"Big deal."

"Anyway, knowing Babes, she don't give a rip about what you think. She pretty strong-minded. Louie, leave them be. I tell you, she ain't all that bad. I like Babes."

"What? Sound like you no care if they—you know, together, like—I mean, I no care if other people be—"

119

"What?" Sterling asks.

"Not Von. She cannot be. She normal."

"Normal?" Sterling laughs. "What if that's what she is? Tell the truth—Von is the most normal, loyal person you know. She one of my best friends. She your sister—"

Right then, the first recess bell rings and Von and I have to hurry to our home ec class. We've already piled up so many tardies, the teacher makes Von and me scrape gum all period sometimes, especially on Fridays when everybody else gets to eat what they make in home ec.

I wait and wait, but Von doesn't come out. I'm about to go get her, but Sterling softly holds on, says wait, just wait, with his hands.

Von comes out walking funny with her head cocked sideways. "What's your problem, Yvonne?" I tell her. "We going get after-school detention with one more tardy. Hurry up." Babes walks out with a tiny purple hickey on her fat neck. I feel sick.

I walk ahead of Von. "Wait, Louie, try wait," Von yells. "I have to tell Babes something." But I don't wait. When Von comes near me, I turn and see a small hickey near the base of her ear, mostly hidden by hair.

I'm so mad, I can't stop myself. "She ain't ever touching you again, you wait, Yvonne," I tell her. "And I hope your mommy and daddy see that thing on you so you can tell them who put it there and what stall you was in."

"Yeah, talk big, Louie. Why no tell Babes?"

"You wait, Yvonne, that's exactly what I going do."

27.
Stone Face

Maybe this ranks as the biggest mistake of my life. I don't know if I do this because I love Von or I hate Babes. I just want to make it stop. I want her back. Lunch recess comes and I go straight to A-building bathroom. I don't wait for Von.

Babes walks past me and blows me off. "What? What you like, shrimp? You ain't no big thing no more. Where *my* other half? Beat it."

She's putting the hickey right in my face. She acts so big when Von or Sterling aren't around. Otherwise, she acts like I'm not there, and that's all right with me. How can she be the so-called friend that Von and Sterling say she is?

Von arrives and bumps me hard from behind. "Oh, sorry, Louie. Mistake. Just like your mistake, not waiting for me. I was waiting outside your English class, punk." The two of them go inside the bathroom.

The door locks shut.

I'm so mad. I'm so hurt. I love you, Von. If you don't know that by now, you're blind and you're more than half stupid, you goddamn Portagee. I have to do this before Sterling arrives. I have to do this now.

I walk into the bathroom through all the thick smoke. I hear one of the titas snipe, "Eh, watch it, stupid Jap." I see Von's shoes. She's sitting on the toilet. I see Babes's shoes. She's standing in front of Von.

By the time I'm slamming my hands on the door of their stall, the whole bathroom's standing behind me ready to see what's going to happen.

"Von, you better come out, right now!" I scream as I slam my hands on the door. "Open this door, c'mon, Von, I begging you. We gotta talk. Von, come out. Please, I begging, come out now."

"Eh, what the haps, man?"

"That's Von's ex-chick?"

"I never know she was going with Von."

"Nah, she nobody to Von."

"She hanging on Sterling—"

"So she bi?"

"What she acting all nuts for?"

"Stupid Jap crybaby."

"Get her out before security come."

"Open the door," I scream. "Open the door, Babes, you fat, ugly, pig-ass sow, you let me in, so I can talk to Yvonne."

That was it.

The door flies open.

Babes comes out raging. "What you said, you little tuna?"

She slams me against the stall door and punches my mouth as I wind her hair around my fist and scratch her face. I kick her in the shins until we both fall to the floor. My mouth cuts open and bleeds onto my clothes before Sterling shoves his way past all the screaming and yelling titas, school security, and the v.p.

"I not finished with you yet," Babes swears as they pull her away from me.

"So what, sow?" I say as she tries to rush me again.

I can't see or hear her very well. But I see Von, before the v.p. takes me out of the bathroom—Von just sitting on the toilet in their stall with her face like stone, looking straight at me.

28.
K for Kyle

"When Uncle Ken them come in a little while, you no say too much about what happen to Emi-Lou, eh, you, Vicky?" my grandma instructs as she stir-fries some dried shrimps.

Grandma's making Thanksgiving dinner. I help her make the sushi rice and get the carrots, eggs, and string beans sliced up to roll inside the nori.

Aunty Vicky's sitting on the La-Z-Boy drinking a Corona with lime from the tree outside. "Why, Ma? You no even know what really happen to her, eh? I was talking to Babes and Viva. They told me some juicy stuffs about this kid. You like know, hah, Ma?" Aunty Vicky sits up in the recliner.

I clean the rice off my hands and go to my room. I don't want my grandma to see my face and know all of this. I hate Aunty Vicky. I look at my black eye in my bureau mirror and the scratches on my cheek scabbing over.

"See you big mouth, Vicky. I know was Kris Hinano wen' buss up Emi-Lou, but you no need be telling Uncle Ken and Aunty Doreen and especially Uncle Charlie and Aunty Etsuko."

"Ma, you never wonder how come Von wasn't there to stop this? From what I hear, Von, Babes, and Louie–one lovers' triangle, I joke you not, Ma. That's what everybody saying about Louie. I told you this before, Ma, she one femme. Louie one lez, Ma."

"You knock that off, Victoria Jean," Grandma says.

"Yeah, whatevers, Ma. Here we go again. I all honest with you and I the one get the blame." The phone ringing breaks up the silence. "Hello? Who? Louie? Yeah, she in her room. Louie, telephone!"

When I answer the call in my grandma's room, it's Sterling. "Hey, Louie-Louie. What you doing?"

"Listening to crap."

"Got one good beat or what?"

"Not funny," I tell him. "My aunty Vicky telling my grandma that I one, that me and Von, we–"

"Tell your grandma that I said for one fact that you *normal*." He laughs.

"Not funny," I tell him again.

"Ho, everything not funny to you. I just playing. Tell your grandma that we, you and me, we–"

"We what?"

"You suppose to figure um out. That was your homework."

"We *friends* then. Since I got only Rudy these days, you gotta be one. But you got Viva, right? No, you more

125

than friends with her." I scribble Sterling's name in cursive on a piece of paper on Grandma's nightstand. I start a *K* for Kyle, then scratch it out.

"Whatever, Louie. You trip me out. Anyway, I was calling to tell you that I was force to go to my mother's house for Thanksgiving."

"Why?"

"Mother and son bonding. I stuck out in Pāhoa. Write this down, Paula Jardine, 928-0907. You going to the party Wailoa tonight? I hope not."

"Probably not. Babes going be there and she said she ain't pau with me yet. I got pounded pretty bad, what you think?"

"Yeah, but you got some licks in with your hair pulling and face scratching," he says. "I bought you some Bactine and judo lessons at my dojo. You got your ass kicked."

"For a good cause," I tell him.

"I told you what I think about all that."

I don't want to hear him side with Von and Babes. "When you coming home?" I ask him.

"I coming back Sunday and I hope by then you looking better—maybe that red blood clot in your eyeball going shrink. Stay green or yellow yet?" Sterling laughs and tells me, "I like call you up late, late tonight so we can talk four, five hours."

"Okay," I tell him. "And put Viva on the line, too."

His voice purrs in my ear. "Just you and me in the dark room, tonight. *Friend.*"

"Promise?" I tease him. As I say this, I think maybe he is my boyfriend. But a friend who is a boy or a boyfriend? I feel even more confused about us.

"Yeah, the dark," he says laughing.

Someone yells at him from another room. "My mother get all these rules on me," he says. "How you like that? Yeah, yeah, yeah," he yells to that someone in the background. "I rather live with my gramma and that's pretty desperate. I call you later, okay? Bye, Louie."

"C'mon, Emi-lou, get off the phone," my grandma yells. "Uncle Ken them just came."

Aunty Doreen carries a huge platter of cake noodles and Uncle has lots of shrimp, shiny red on a blue Chinese plate. Then Uncle Charlie, Aunty Etsuko, and Von arrive. My small cousins, Cori and Travis, come in with our aunty Nancy. First thing she says is, "Ho, what happen to your eye, Emi-lou?"

"Grandma buss you up? That's what you get when you lip off at my Godzilla sista, right, Reiko?" Uncle Ken laughs.

Von's sitting on the couch by herself. I stare at her, daring her to tell them all what happened. She just stares back.

"What wall you walked into?" Aunty Doreen asks, breaking the tension. "Gunfunnit, you look like crap, Emi-lou. What happen to this kid, Lea?"

"Whoa, baby, he ain't worth it if he busses you up like that. I take him by the ears, swing that boyfriend of yours around the room, and kick his butt out the door. I tell you, no man, I repeat, no man ever give me lickins and live to see the sun rise the next day." Everybody laughs at this because Aunty Nancy's so big, she busted up her ex-husband and her new boyfriend more than a few times each.

Halfway through dinner, Babes's truck comes screeching up our driveway. Von gets up to go. "And where you think you going, Yvonne Shigeko Vierra?" Uncle Charlie asks.

"No call me that, sheez. I told you, Daddy, the girls all going down Wailoa after their Thanksgiving dinner."

"Well, I no think you going unless Emi-lou go to keep an eye on you. 'Cause where Yvonne go–" The whole room finishes blandly–"Emi-lou go."

Von looks at me hard. I've never seen her look at me like that before. She's saying, but not with words. *You better get up right now and go with me like nothing's wrong, or I'm going to hate you more.*

Aunty Vicky pulls on her Hilo Astros jacket. "Why? I going, Uncle Charlie. I watch Von for you guys."

"You?" Grandma chimes in. "Sorry, my dear, but I trust Emi-lou with Yvonne more than you." My grandma looks at me. "You sure you want to go, Emi-lou? Don't let us force you."

I look at Von and nod a small yes.

"Yeah, yeah, yeah," Aunty Vicky mutters from the porch. "C'mon, you guys. Like Babes leave us?" I hurry out the door. Von climbs in the truck and Aunty Vicky gets in behind her. "I ain't freezing my ass back there," Aunty Vicky grumbles. "Get in the back, Louie, you hound from hell." They all laugh when she starts barking like a dog.

At the last pavilion at Wailoa, I see everybody's cars. There's lots of coolers and pupus. Anita lights a cigarette. Choochie and Rae share a bottle of Bay Rum. Genevieve sits by Sissy Miyamoto. Sissy Miyamoto?

Since when do she and her friends party with all the girls? Kyle, Levi, Melvin, and the whole boys' volleyball team's there, except for Sterling.

Kyle squeezes his butt between Sissy and Viva. He kisses them both and says, "My concubine." I never knew he had a three-syllable word in his whole vocabulary.

I sit way on the side by Rae, Anita, and Rudy.

"Hey, girl, looking like Sugar Ray Leonard. You tell Uncle Rudy the whole story from beginning to end," he says, "'cause what I heard through the grapevine was pretty juicy." He puts his skinny arm around me.

Kyle walks over and kneels next to me. "Eh, I like talk to you. Just you and me while Sterling not here."

"I know what your English deadline is," I whisper. Anita turns and looks at me.

"Um-hum," Rudy says with tightly pursed lips. "U-ser."

"Shhh, big mouth," Kyle slurs. "And you, you fa—" he says to Rudy, stopping when Anita and Rae turn his way. "Was I talking to you?"

"You only nice to me when you need something. Go away," I tell him.

"A-men, sista Louie," Rudy adds.

"Typical," Anita chimes in, "typical man."

"Come, Louie. Come with me to my car," Kyle whispers right into my ear. "I like tell you what Sterling told me about you. You know, his *true* feelings. Private," he says jerking his eyebrows at me. "He like me be the one tell you something, something personal."

"I just talked to him—" I turn toward Anita, who

gives Kyle a stink-eye. Rudy listens intently.

"He called me half hour ago. He like me tell you tonight."

"Where your car?" I ask him. He points by lifting his cocky chin to the far side of the parking lot.

"Hurry up, then." Rudy takes my hand in his for a moment, then he lets me go. I turn around as we walk away and see both Sissy and Viva looking at us like they're jealous. I start feeling justified inside. I know that's sick of me, but that's what I feel. Good. Good for them. Anyway, he just wants to talk to me about Sterling.

Kyle pushes the front seat forward and makes me climb in the back. "I getting low *D*s in social studies," he says.

"What? What about Sterling?" I ask.

"He like Viva. All the boys telling him to check her out," Kyle tells me. "I like you write this ten-page extra-credit paper on the illegal overthrow of the Hawaiian monarchy."

"Who told you?" I ask him.

"Sterling. Yesterday. I mean today. He told me and Baron to fix him up." Kyle moves closer to me.

"I thought he said something about me half-hour ago, you liar."

"Nah, easy, Emi-lou. Miss Murai said she give me one *C* if I do um good, and if I don't, I on the borderline *D* or *F*. And if I fail social studies—"

I don't respond. I'm getting sick of this. All the lies. All the rumors going round and round. "But Sterling just told me—"

"He lie," Kyle says. "He like Viva. And all the boys like him going with Viva. So what? You going help me?"

Stupid. Just plain stupid. Kyle could've just asked me this in front of all of them. No, he has too much pride. He doesn't want them to think he needs a nobody like me.

"Well? Answer, dammit!" Kyle yells. "I ain't got all night." Then he acts all nice again. "Like go cruising with me so you can think it over? I tell you what Sterling told me the other day. About you, not Viva. You like go Four Miles or Isles?"

"Nah, not really," I tell him.

"Then maybe this going help." Kyle's drunk. He's being rough and mean till finally he puts his hand over my mouth.

"Stop it!" I scream.

"Shut up, Emi-lou, I know you like this from me. Sterling no give this to you so you can get it from me." His hand leaves a taste in my mouth of Ralph Lauren Polo and rum. My head hits the side of the car as Kyle pushes me down. I can't breathe.

He pins my flailing arms. What's going on? Let go of my mouth. I must be screaming. I taste his cologne down my throat, Polo, thick and heavy, a taste all over my mouth, and I gag.

He starts hiking my skirt up and I panic. "No make noise, Emi-lou, they might think you don't want it. You want it?" Kyle starts breathing hard. His hand moves down, down. And then he struggles to unbuckle his belt, Kyle struggling with his zipper, pushing on me hard.

Then glass shatters. The windshield breaks open. A baseball bat comes through twice. "Let her go!" All the girls come running. "Let her go!" Von screams as she kicks the car, pounding its sides with the bat.

I come scrambling out of the backseat. I straighten my skirt. "My mother's car!" Kyle screams as he charges Von.

She cocks the bat and starts moving it in slow circles, the way she poises at the plate when she's thinking about where she wants to hit the ball.

Rae and Chooch grab him from behind. Anita's holding Rudy back.

"C'mon, c'mon, punk!" Von yells as she drops the bat. "Why no tell everybody how come you get good grades nowadays, you stupid dummy? Tell Sissy, c'mon, Kyle."

Kyle tries to rush Von. But Levi and Melvin step between them as Rae and Chooch pull him away from Von. He's swinging and swearing as Babes tries to calm him. She turns and reaches her hand out to Von.

But she yanks herself away from Babes, picks up the bat, and looks around for me. I'm sitting on the curb, curled up in a ball and shivering. She gives me the head jerk, let's go, then helps me get up. We start walking out of the park.

"Wait, wait, Von," Babes yells, "Let me take you home."

"Take care your cuz," Von says.

"I call you tonight. Talk this out, Von. C'mon, we said we not going ever go home mad. We more than this."

Von puts her arm around me. "You okay, Louie-Louie? Answer me. You all right?" Von's crying with me and saying over and over, "You okay? You okay? He nothing, Louie. Nothing, you hear me?"

I nod and repeat her words, which sink into me like motion sickness. "He nothing. You right. He make me sick."

"I take care of you—so you no need tell nobody what wen' happen," Von says as she strokes my hair. "Nobody but me."

Von and I walk home in the cold night, the black sky smooth above us, Von holding my head to her chest, and cars passing slowly on Manono Street.

29.
The Waters of
Leleiwi

When I wake up the next morning, Von's sleeping beside me on the living room floor. I take my warm futon and tuck it under her neck. She makes a snorking mumble then turns the other way. Sunlight moves across her face. The phone rings and I pick it up before it disturbs Von's sleep.

"So what, Louie-girl, you all right?" Rudy asks. He's angry and concerned. "Call the cops. Turn him in. Who he think he is? They all pissed at him," he jabbers on.

"Who that?" Von asks, her voice morning-hoarse.

"Rudy," I tell her.

"Ask him if he going beach with us today," Von says, "and tell him we riding our bikes so no complain."

"I heard," Rudy grumbles. "Tell Von I treating her breakfast, I mean the McDonald's Big Breakfast, 'cause she the man, the kick-ass hero of the year. Good for Kyle, that prick."

"Rudy said to tell you–" I begin, mildly irritated. "You guys like talk to each other?" I ask Von, holding the phone out to her.

Von takes it. "No be late. We leaving in one hour," she tells him, handing the phone back to me then pulling the futon over her head.

"No worry, honey-boom, I already put on all my makeup," he says, "and I slept in my Speedos 'cause nothing like the feel of Lycra on my red satin sheets."

"It's me, Rudy," I tell him.

"Oh. See you," he trails off.

We sit on the craggy lava rocks at Leleiwi, sea grass moving stiff arms, the pull and swirl of water in a small tidal pool beside us. Nobody speaks for a long time. It's like what happened to me happened to all of us. I feel dirty and used.

"My aunty Anita told me," Rudy begins.

"What?" I ask.

"You need to go into the saltwater and cleanse yourself of all this. And you gotta walk out backward from the ocean."

Von chuckles. She dangles her feet in the warm tidal pool. Little hermit crabs skitter away.

"What?" Rudy whines. "She said it make all the negativity ions dis-perse in the uni-verse."

Von laughs again.

"Louie-dahling, Uncle Rudy's always in poetry mode, don't you notice?" He dives into the water. "See," he yells. "Poof! All my sadness gone!" He swims out toward a little island. I watch him get smaller and smaller.

There's a rough kind of wind in the orange sky. And no real words to tell Von what I feel about what she did for me. "Von, man, you put me before Babes," I begin awkwardly. "Thanks." I hold out my hand to her.

She looks at my hand, draws her knees in to her chest, and sighs. "I going tell you straight," she says at last.

"What?"

"Seem like we get this whole ocean between us." She looks out at the sea mist in the ironwood trees. "And the way you react to what I tell you–" she warns.

I feel scared. I know what's coming. I watch Rudy sunning himself on the little island. I want him to come back, to make this easier, to make us laugh.

"Just tell me, Von."

She takes a deep breath. "Me and Babes, we–"

"I know," I interrupt.

Von lowers her gaze. Her jaw tightens but she continues. "We way more than friends. You gotta just accept it, Louie."

I say nothing.

"That's just the way it is. You can be all right with that?"

She's not asking me, she's telling me. I shrug my shoulders.

"I mean, no change nothing between me and you is what I trying to say."

"Yeah, right," I mutter. "So far, Babes changed a lot of things between us."

"C'mon, Louie, cut me some slack. I would do the

same for you if you and Sterling wanted to spend time with each other. And you always doing things with Rudy, without me."

"Not the same," I tell Von. I pick up a piece of coral and fling it into the water.

"Why? 'Cause me and Babes both girls? And we, you know, together?"

"Maybe. I thought you was pau with her. I mean, after what *her cousin* did to me last night–"

"But wasn't her," Von says.

I want to cry, but I don't. I reach deeper inside me. "You always taking her side over mine. I thought we was V-a-L?"

"We are. But now, I get her. We tight, Louie, like me and you but in a different way. And you gotta deal. You just gotta."

"I would never do that to you, Von, never. Take Sterling's side or Rudy's side over you? Never. That's pretty weak, you know that?"

Von looks up at me. "It ain't about taking sides." She pauses. "But I tell you what. Me and you, we blood. You my number one girl, always. But you gotta take Babes in as part of me. You can?"

Von looks at me with those eyes. I've always broken her with my words. "Maybe," I say at last. "Maybe, yeah." Von leans in toward me, our bodies touching. "Okay, I can try," I whisper.

"And promise me, Louie, promise–you ain't saying nothing to my mother and father, your grandma, nobody. And last night," she says. "I ain't telling nobody. You gotta promise me."

I give her a slow nod.

"You get your fingers or toes crossed?" Von asks.

I shake my head. The wind flutters my hair. "Deep," I tell her at last.

Von sighs. "Deeper than the deep blue sea."

"Let's get rid of our negative eyeballs." Von laughs as she dives into the water. I watch Rudy ease himself into the water. He swims toward us.

I dive into the cold seawater.

"Ready for the cleansing, ladies," Rudy says, taking our hands. "On the count of three, we submerge the polluted shells of our human existence in the healing waters of Leleiwi–"

"Oh, cut the drama," Von complains. "One," she counts.

"A-two," Rudy flourishes.

"Three," I finish.

And the water envelops us, cool and forgiving.

30.
More Than Friends

As soon as I step into newswriting class, Mrs. Hatayama sends me to the student gov office for the results of the Homecoming Royal Court. I'm to write the story as soon as the ballots are all counted.

Homecoming King is Rex Koʻohonu, and the Queen is Angela Matsuo. He plays volleyball and basketball. She paddles canoe and surfs.

Senior attendants–Pono Kunishima and Marisa Sue Pang. He's a nationally ranked karate champion and she's a varsity cheerleader who's on the water polo team.

The junior dreamboat is Kyle Kiyabu and his sweetheart, Sissy Miyamoto. He's a punk and she's a pus on a punk.

Sophomore dreamboat, I knew this was going to happen–Sterling Jardine. He's the best setter in the league and a shooting guard on the basketball team. But his sweetheart–I knew this would happen, too–is Genevieve Ching. I don't even write down the names of the freshman attendants.

"This mean they go with each other to the Homecoming Ball?" I ask the student gov advisor like it's a question for my article.

"Of course," she says like I should've known, and she had better things to do than explain this to a freshman of all insignificant lowlifes.

It's not that I want to go to the Homecoming Ball, because I really don't. I'm not afraid of Sterling doing something stupid with Viva. Or maybe I am. I just think it's not fair. I can just hear Viva telling all the softball girls, "Good for Louie, stupid big mouth copycat. Watch me score Sterling—and after a taste of Viva Two-Percent-Angel, he ain't ever going back to that generic nobody brand."

That afternoon, my grandma senses my sadness even when I hide it in that quiet place that only Von knows about. "On the night of the Twilight Rally," Grandma suggests, "tell Sterling and Yvonne come over for dinner and we can take pictures of you folks, okay, Emi-lou?"

I hesitate. I'd rather avoid the whole thing. When Sterling calls me that night at seven-thirty like he always does, Grandma picks up the phone and tells him herself. "So tomorrow night, be here at about six o'clock. Pick up Yvonne on your way over. Me and Emi-lou make a nice dinner for all us."

"I go with you to the Twilight Rally," Grandma tells me after she hangs up the phone. "We bring Sterling a nice puakenikeni lei, three strand, you like?"

She knows I have nobody to go with after Von's proclamation of "No dorky school-related affairs for me but you can go all you like, Louie."

"Rudy and me sewed a satin banner in home ec class for the homecoming banner competition," I tell her. "He said he stay with me at the Twilight Rally for the results."

"Rudy Rudman?" She seems a little hurt. "Well, I pick you guys up after all pau. Sterling gotta take the Ching girl home, right? Call me from the pay phone outside the Civic Auditorium."

Sterling looks so handsome in his black tux. Von combs his hair using her expensive salon gel. He has that flush in his face that he gets when he comes out of the locker room after a game. My grandma takes pictures of me giving him the three strands of puak-enikeni—about twelve shots. Aunty Vicky and Von get in some of the pictures.

He talks easily with my grandma like they've known each other all their lives, and my aunty Vicky doesn't smart-mouth him either. Von hadn't told him about what happened with Kyle, so Sterling's been really curious as to why we're close again.

Last weekend, Sterling wanted to see *Exorcist I, II* and *III* at the Plaza but I didn't want to, so he and Grandma went together. They played golf a couple of afternoons with Aunty Etsuko. Grandma even let Sterling smoke if he wanted.

"I going rent spooky movies," he says as Grandma straightens his bow tie. "All the *Friday the Thirteenths*, and me and you go watch all night next Friday, Mrs. Kaya."

"I like watch, too," Aunty Vicky says. "Louie can go

her room and play with her Chucky dolls, right Louie?"

"Ha. Ha," I tell her. "Very funny."

"She forgot to laugh," Von deadpans.

"Wise up, two losers—I could tell some real spooky stories about Wailoa, get my drift?" Aunty Vicky says.

"What?" Sterling asks. "Something happened? Eh, whassup?" he whispers to Von.

"Nothing," she says.

"Yeah, right. You and Louie better 'fess up," he says.

When dinner's finished and Sterling's about to go, Grandma tells him, "You look for Emi-lou in the stands, okay, Sterling?" She's looking at me, trying to locate my sadness.

"No worry," he says. "Laters, Von—why no go with Louie to the rally?"

"What I said about dorkiness? No thanks." She laughs. "I get other plans."

"Like what?" I ask.

"Like other plans, okay?" Von's not totally the same with me, but at least she's here.

When Sterling and I go outside, it's already dark, and he takes me to the driver's side of his truck. He kisses me, moving his tongue inside my mouth, and his hand slides up my back. "No worry, okay?" he says. "Viva is Viva. This is baby-sitting to me."

I feel light-headed, as though my legs have turned into taffy. "Okay," I mumble before I completely melt into the asphalt.

"We more than friends," he says.

31.
The Twilight Rally

Rudy Rudman always dresses all out when we do things like this, just because he's the Hilo Intermediate student government president. "We might win the banner competition, dude, 'cause that banner was designed by Rude," he tells me. "That's why I simply must look sharp when I pick up the trophy on stage in the spotlight, honey."

"Shake yo' booty, Rudy," I tell him. "In the nudey—"

"Please don't get crudey," he snaps as he walks toward the doors of the Civic Auditorium. "Now follow Uncle Rudy."

At the Twilight Rally, the junior and senior housebands do a Battle of the Bands, the flag girl corps from the marching band performs, the cheerleaders do all kinds of dances like they're the L.A. Laker Girls. They announce the winners of the float competition first and the banner next. Rudy takes second place and screams and carries on in the spotlight until the principal escorts him off the stage.

And then the lights dim in the Civic Auditorium. The shiny mirrored ball starts spinning and the lights flash from the DJ's platform on the stage. The Homecoming Court has to dance to the theme song, "I'll Always Love You."

Genevieve looks so sexy in her red dress, all shiny and backless with her red satin gloves. Her hair falls softly around her face and a tiara sits perched on her head. Sterling helps her down the wooden stage and onto the gym floor.

He knows where I'm sitting and after he puts his arms around her, he waves to me. "Ai, ai, um-hum, check him out, Louie, girlfriend. Arms around another wo-man. Three snaps around the world for big zero zaps to him," Rudy says.

"He had to, stupid," I tell Rudy.

"Um-hum," he says, "boy don't have to make like he catching such major thrills. Too close, girl," he yells at Genevieve, "back off, um-hum, you heard, back off."

"We more than friends," I tell him.

"Um-hum, show proof. Poof. None found."

"I don't care. Promise."

"A word made to be broken, *promise*, that is," Rudy says with another snap.

I just thought that this could be like the movies if I prayed hard enough. I should know better. Nothing is ever like the movies.

It would be easy for Sterling to get Levi to dance the rest of the song with Viva and then come up the stands and get me. I'm looking at Sterling and he's looking at me. I'm telling him with my mind, "Come get me," over and over.

The song ends, and he escorts Viva back to her wicker chair on the wooden stage. Pretty soon, the court leaves and disappears into the locker room. Viva's smiling big like a Miss Congeniality and her hair's golden-brown like she retinted her whole head.

At the end of the Twilight Rally, I sit outside by the pay phone in front of the Civic with Rudy and he's talking away about Gloria Estefan and the Miami Sound Machine and how his cousin is in a band who can sing just like Gloria and Emilio, especially "Do the Conga." I see Babes's truck first, followed by Sterling's truck. None of them sees me. There's someone in the truck with Babes. Von? They sit close together. Sterling and Viva sit cut-seat, two-heads-one-driver. They head toward Wailoa, Viva's house, in the other direction.

32.

Accusations

I pick up the phone.

"Who you calling?" Grandma asks.

"Sterling."

"No tie up the line, you hear me? Keep it short." She steps out on the lanai to tend to her dendrobiums.

I saw you with Viva after the Twilight Rally last night, I practice in my head. Rudy and me saw you sitting cut-seat. Where did you go? What did you do with Viva? I practice these words with anger. Accusation. Self-pity. Mild curiosity. Possessiveness.

If things were back to normal between Von and me, she would rehearse and coach me. No, too babyish. Too jealous. Make him think. Hint, just hint. Okay, try mad. Let me milk his mind first. This is deep, Louie-Louie, deeper than the deep blue sea.

I shove two Chips Ahoy in my mouth and then another. Von hasn't been shoplifting diet pills for me lately. And since that night at Wailoa, I've been hungry. All the time.

I dial. "Sterling?"

"That's you, Louie? Why so soft?"

"Rudy and me seen you and Viva last night sitting cut-seat going to Wailoa." It comes out as a rushed blurt in monotone. Cookie crumbs fall out of my mouth. So much for mental rehearsal.

"Whoa, wait now. What?"

"You heard. Who else was there? Jerk."

"Me and Baron. Kyle was there. Levi and Spence. Yeah, Sissy and Viva. Von was with Babes. I had a beer. I took her home. The end."

"Von? That was her other plans? Why couldn't she just tell me?" I feel hurt. "So, Viva tried to—"

"Of course, Louie, all night. You know Viva."

"Just like you hiding me and showing them her," I whisper. "You shame of me. I no blame you. I would hide me, too. Von was at the rally with Babes? She could've come with me and Rudy." I feel hungrier. This time for something salty.

"C'mon, now, Louie—"

"Emi-lou," Grandma calls from the lanai, "ask Sterling if he need one more two-for-one coupon for rent the spooky movies tonight."

"You wrong," he says, "about me and Viva."

"And tell him no need bring snacks," she says waving a dead orchid clipping. "He look so handsome last night."

"Yeah, handsome," I repeat.

"I see you tonight. I ain't hiding you, Louie."

"Whatever," I tell him. "You wait, brah." I hang up the phone.

33.
Hunger

Sterling comes over with Von that night. He rented all the *Child's Play* movies for Grandma to watch with him. She makes all kinds of mochi crunch snacks, Chex party mix, and Sterling's favorite, clam dip with Fritos.

Aunty Vicky's on the La-Z-Boy with her legs spread all over the armrests as usual. "No wonder you no more boyfriend, Vicks," Sterling tells her. "Too many flies."

"He the one with the flies all around him," I mutter.

Aunty Vicky throws a cashew at his head, and he picks it up off the ground. "No more five seconds on the floor, so no more germs," he says as he pops it in his mouth. "Screw um if they cannot take a joke, yeah, Louie?"

"Whatever."

"No more germs, Sterling, just everybody's toe jams for the last twenty years," Grandma says as she throws some zabutons on the floor and spreads a heavy futon for all of us to lie down on in front of the TV.

I grab a handful of party mix and stuff it in my mouth. Von throws a stink-eye at me for being so uncool to Sterling. "Louie," she says, "can you get me my futon from your room?"

"Get it yourself," I tell her.

"No, you come with me and we both get it," she says, yanking me off the floor. She grabs her backpack and heads down the hall. When we get to my room, she pushes me in.

"Why you acting like such a bitch, man?" she asks me. I turn off the light. Von turns it back on. "Well?"

"I saw him and Viva last night sitting cut-seat. They went to Wailoa. And you and Babes. How come you didn't come to the rally with me and Rudy?" I plop down on my bed and put my pillow over my stomach.

"What we just talk about?" Von asks. "Sometimes I like do things with Babes, just me and her."

"All the time," I grumble.

"I trying so hard to make things right with you and with her, then with you, then with her, you know what, Louie, I getting sick of this crap going around and around in circles."

"And Sterling and Viva, you think–" I cannot even get the words out. "I so hungry, Von. I gaining weight 'cause all this."

"You better shape up, Louie," Von says as she throws a teddy bear at my head. "I was right there. He did nothing with Viva. Yeah, she was trying, but he was pushing her off all night. Get a grip."

"What you girls doing?" Grandma yells down the hall. "We like start the movie."

"We coming," Von answers. She reaches for her backpack. "Here, laxatives all week. Was all I could get. The old lady almost busted me." She throws the box at me.

I don't care what Von said. I'm so mad at Sterling. But it's like he's become a part of our family. A nephew, cousin, or brother. A more-than-friend. My anger and hurt begin to dissolve. He's here with us, not her. And Von's here with me, not Babes.

Sterling folds a zabuton in half and tucks it under his chest as he lays down next to me on his stomach. "Louie, you stay and watch all night with us, okay?" he says, bumping his shoulder into mine. "If come spooky, close your eyes and ears and sing so you drown out what Chucky saying."

After the first few gore and slash scenes, Aunty Vicky pauses the VCR and says, "No need sing so loud. Make her do something else, Sterling. Emi-lou, you ruining the movie. Ma, make her go to her room."

She presses play. I scream and bury my face in Von's shoulder. "I going get nightmares."

"I sleeping over, gee whiz, no need get all scared. Pass me the bean dip, Sterling. I fut Chucky out of our room when he come tonight."

"Whoa, killa wiffa." Sterling laughs.

At about twelve-thirty, all the tapes finish. Grandma says good night and Aunty Vicky follows her down the hallway. "Let's sneak onto the back nine late tomorrow afternoon," she tells Sterling. "Me, you, Yvonne, and Ets."

"Shoots, Louie caddy for me," he says. "We play for money, okay?"

"You pay up, now. After I kick your ass." Grandma laughs. "Good night."

I walk Sterling to his truck. "You going tell me what happened?" he asks me.

"Nothing," I tell him.

"C'mon," he says, "how come you and Von friends again?"

"Nothing, I told you. You deaf? Nothing happened, my more-than-a-friend friend who was with Viva Ching."

"No change the subject. Get this buzzing going around, and funny, but nobody like tell me nothing. And how come Von and Babes was mad at each other?"

"I don't know. They not mad now." To tell him why would take him to Kyle and me in the car.

He starts apologizing about the Twilight Rally thing. He promises we can iron things out. Nothing happened, so he says. Viva insisted on sitting close to him like that. He kept pushing her off. It's over. I don't believe him.

"Okay, good night, Louie. Sorry." He leans into me as he presses my back against the truck, his hands behind my neck, his breathing shallow; he runs his hands down my back and moves his tongue with mine, over my teeth, and licks and sucks my lips.

I believe him.

34.
My Own Whole Face

Roxanne's coming home for New Year's. In fact, she and my aunty Amy both plan on coming home. I don't even care. It's cruel of me to feel this way, but to me, she's not my mother. My grandma's my mother and she's just Roxanne, somebody who happened to give birth to me.

The night before Roxanne arrives, Grandma lays down the law. "Vicky, you better not say nothing about Roxanne when she come home, you hear me?" she starts. "We all be pleasant so that she stays in Hilo with us and not Pāhoa with what's-his-name."

"Jerry, Ma, Jerry Rapoza," Vicky says. "I bet he be at the airport waiting for Rocky come home. And Ma, what about Louie, you better give her some laws, too. I lonesome being the only one with rules."

Grandma looks at me kindly. "Emi-lou," she whispers, then pauses for a long time. "Expect nothing from your mother, okay? She got very little to give."

I know what Grandma's saying. She's not talking

about late Christmas presents. She's talking about Roxanne's selfish self.

"She was always like this?" I ask.

"No," Grandma says.

"Yes," Aunty Vicky says.

"Was my fault," Grandma says as she puts on her Keds. "Easier being a grandma than a mother. I was rough on all my girls. I had to be or they step all over me. I never let your mother be who she was. Was my way or the highway."

"So Rocky hit the road," Aunty Vicky adds. "Lucky thing I not bonehead like Rocky, yeah, Ma?"

"You one whole different story," Grandma says. "I just feel bad for Emi-lou."

"And it's always about Emi-lou," Aunty Vicky grumbles.

Grandma ignores her. "You the only bridge between us and that's a bad place to be."

When we pick up Roxanne at the Hilo airport, I feel anxious. My grandma passes me the puakenikeni leis. Roxanne comes down the escalator to the baggage claim and we wave at her. Grandma holds out her arms to my mother, as she acts like she doesn't see us in the crowd of people—and heads straight for a handsome man with long hair pulled back in a ponytail.

She's being mean on purpose. It's got to be that, or maybe she's just plain dumb. "Jerry, Jerry," she coos as they kiss. This has got to be the biggest act for the three of us standing there like big dummies with our jaws dropped and gaping open.

Jerry walks over to us. "Eh, howzit, Vicky," he says as he gives her a slap on the back. "Mrs. Kaya, Happy

New Year." He pecks Grandma's cheek. "And who dis? That's you, Emi-lou? Wow, you wen' really pull down."

"I gained some back," I tell him.

"Ho, I swear, you look *just like your mother.*"

I cringe. Roxanne streaks her hair with blonde highlights. She's wearing blue and pink eyeshadow with heavy eyeliner, she's got six holes in each ear, and her fingernails are so long, they look like red claws with sequins and gold stripes. Her lip gloss looks like it might drip down her shirt and she's chewing gum like it's too wet for her tiny mouth to handle. She's wearing an armful of jangling Hawaiian bracelets. I hope I never look like her.

But all the same, I can't help thinking, Why's my mother ignoring me? Why doesn't she say hi or hug me or act like I'm there at least? Maybe, like Grandma says, I shouldn't expect anything from her. Did my grandma really mean to expect absolutely *nothing*?

"How old you now, Emi-lou?" Jerry asks. "What grade you in? I swear, just like Rocky when she was in high school."

This is when Roxanne breaks in. "Maybe she looks like me, a little, but I had bigger boobs. Emi-lou, you're what, twelve? No, thirteen and in seventh? No wait, eighth grade, right, Mom?"

"Ninth," Grandma says. I know she's trying hard not to grit her teeth when she talks.

"Jeez, time flies when you're in beauty school then breaking your back to eke out a living." She pecks my cheek to act close, mother-daughter, because Jerry's been paying some attention to me.

I see my reflection in the glass door. Something comes over me. I look at Roxanne and Jerry standing there and I see my own face. I don't know why I never saw this before. I've seen them in lots of pictures—proms, May Day, graduation.

My own whole face.

Like when Uncle Ken holds my cousin Travis, he looks like him. When Aunty Doreen holds him, he looks like her. But when you put the three of them together, you see Travis's face in both of their faces.

Like now. I *know* he's my father, right there. And something tightens up inside me.

35.
Just Like Old Times

We have dinner at Restaurant Fuji, fill gas at Fat's 76, buy pastries at Lanky's, and rent videotapes. That's pretty much the last I see of my mother. She knows we planned to spend New Year's Eve with all of us Kayas at Grandma's, "just like old times."

Aunty Amy arrives from New York City with a haole boyfriend named Tate who has white feet. Aunty Vicky's pissed off because the girls are partying down at Wailoa but she's forced to spend New Year's Eve at home. That and no Roxanne.

"Call the Hukilau Hotel," Aunty Vicky grumbles to Grandma. "That's where Jerry staying for couple more days. Catching up for lost time."

Aunty Amy rolls her eyes like she's way better than Vicky, the tita, Roxanne, the slut, and me, the bastard. Tate puts his haole arm around Aunty Amy like, "That's okay. You've moved on and elevated your station in life. You are better than they are."

Right, Aunty Amy, the haole wanna-be.

"Shut up, Vicky," Grandma hisses. "See what I mean? What you insinuating about Roxanne right in front of Emi-lou? I swear, you got no class whatsoever." Grandma takes a long look out the picture window.

"No matter to me," I whisper.

"No talk like that about your mother," Grandma says.

"Why?" Aunty Vicky retorts. "You do."

"You listen to me, Victoria Jean—" Grandma begins.

"Mom—let's not lose our cool. After all, the rest of us are here—Tate and I, though a little jet-lagged—Vicky, you, and Emi-lou. It's not quite yet twelve and dinner's got to digest." Aunty Amy talks so haole with her sassy mouth and sassy eyes. "Besides, even if Roxanne doesn't make it home by twelve, Emi-lou won't mind, right, Emi? I mean, you consider Granny more like your—"

Why do they make things so ugly, all of them. I hate my aunty Amy. She thinks she's so big time, living in New York City and coming home every couple of years to act high and mighty.

"Yeah, Grandma's my mother. So what?" I snap at her. "Who been here with Grandma since Grandpa died? Not you."

"You watch your mouth, Emi-lou," Aunty Amy scolds.

For a long time after he died, it was only Grandma, Aunty Vicky, and me. But it was okay. Every New Year's Eve, Grandma and I took a hot shot of sake with cocoa-back. And it was me who insisted on sticking to Grandpa's tradition of lighting the ten thousand Duck-brand firecrackers on the tall bamboo pole at midnight. I wanted tonight to be no different.

Close to eleven o'clock, Grandma starts getting real mad. "Take two shots sake, Emi-lou," she says, "so you sleep good. And Lord knows you going need some help tonight. Vicky, find Roxanne's envelope to Emi-lou."

"What envelope?" I begin to say.

"The card she gave me at the airport," Grandma says.

"Where did you put it?" Aunty Vicky asks, shuffling through a pile of envelopes on the dining room table. She finds it at last and passes it to Grandma.

"Open it now," Grandma says slowly. "In front all us and Grandpa, too. Pour him one shot, Amy." Aunty Amy pours a shot of sake and puts it in front of Grandpa's picture on the TV.

I turn it over in my hands with a grimace.

"Open that envelope," Grandma says again.

I open it very slowly. Inside, I find a Christmas card with white glitter. Twenty bucks and the card's signed, "To: Emi-lou, From: Mommy and Uncle Jerry."

"Goddammit," Grandma swears.

"Mommy?" I tell her.

"Uncle Jerry? Please," Grandma goes on. "What's the matter with her? Roxanne get the gall to put money in a cheap hundred-for-dollar Christmas card."

"You spoiled her, Mom," Aunty Amy starts, "just like Dad did. And when she got promiscuous and pregnant–"

"You was too strict with her," Aunty Vicky says.

"Don't you dare talk like that about your father," Grandma says. "We did the best we knew how. You all knew your options if you ever got pregnant–"

"What options?" Aunty Vicky asks sarcastically.

"Oh stop it, Vicky, you know exactly what Mom's talking about," Aunty Amy says.

I walk away from the bickering to my room and close the door behind me. I don't cry, so that they leave me alone. Why does she hate me so much? My own stupid mother. What's wrong with her?

What's wrong with *me*? Too ugly. Too stupid. Too fat.

After everybody gets to sleep, I go back outside into the living room. It's three o'clock in the morning and I'm still awake. I hear a car pull into our driveway. Roxanne shuts the car door softly. She creeps into the house. She smells like she's breathing liquor.

She stops and looks at me. I pretend to be asleep on the couch. Pretty soon, she takes her small suitcase with her. She stops to look at me again. I open my eyes and see her back, her golden hair, leave through the back door of our house.

36.
None of the Above

Grandma's whispering on the phone. "You see, that's what I mean about you, Roxanne. You one selfish, spoiled girl. You only think about yourself. This kid don't even know who her damn father is and she get one invisible mother on top of that.

"And what the hell is this, giving her twenty bucks? Was that her Christmas gift from you? 'Gee thanks, maybe I can go buy my own gift from the after-Christmas sales at the mall.'

"And when you coming back into town? No think Emi-lou going Pāhoa, 'cause I ain't driving her. You should've think of taking her with you when you left on New Year's Eve.

"No, going be too late. Emi-lou's going with the volleyball team to Honolulu for the state tournament. Tomorrow. No, too late, Roxanne. By the time Emi-lou come back you be long gone.

"See what you done? You father was right when he said all you good for is break our heart. Abortion, no.

Adoption, no. When you chose none of the above, you made the most cruel decision. Roxanne? Roxanne?"

My grandma hangs up the phone. She's probably crying out there and wiping her eyes with her T-shirt. I finally understand Roxanne's *options*. To Grandma and Grandpa, I wasn't an option. But Roxanne chose none of the above. She had me out of rebellion and spite.

I feel a cold sweat come over me. I dial Von's number from the phone in Grandma's room. "Eh, hi, Louie. Happy New Year, and all that." Von's the only person I can talk to honestly about my mother. "Whassup?" Von asks. "Where you was last night? All us was down Wailoa. Louie?"

"Von, my mother, she ain't here no more. She went Pāhoa with Jerry and 'cause we going Honolulu tomorrow, I ain't going see her already. I kinda feeling like–"

"Sorry, Louie. About your mom, this is deep, man, deeper than the deep blue sea–"

"I wasn't an option to my mother," I blurt. "And about Sterling and Viva–Von, you sure what you told me? He trying to convince me that–" The Wonder-Phone breaks in to our line.

"Try wait, Louie." The phone clicks and there's silence for a while. "Louie, that's Babes on the other line. I call you back later on. We going get some stuffs for the Honolulu trip at Longs Drugs. Like go?"

"But–"

"But what? You like go?"

"Nah. Thanks, Von."

"You all right, right? I mean, I can call you up after I come back from Longs."

I don't say anything. How can she leave me hanging like this? If I accepted her and Babes, didn't she say I'd always be her number one?

"I going sleep your house tonight anyways 'cause they playing poker. Louie? You all right?"

"Maybe, I mean, no. I mean, whatever—"

"I gotta go. We made plans, me and Babes. I talk to you tonight, promise. Bye."

I hang up the phone and feel the empty space of the room grow big and vibrate like waves as my body crumbles. I hear my grandma crying in the living room. What did I expect?

37.
Be-cuz

At the Big Island Interscholastic Federation volleyball awards, Mr. Robert Teixeira, our athletic director, called us up on stage with the team. "These four girls," he announced, "lent an air of first class to the team with their hustle and exquisite grooming." After the ceremony, Mr. Teixeira told Coach Huggie that he would provide four round-trip tickets for the girls to accompany the team to Honolulu. But Von's amazing organization was the sole reason the statisticians got to go.

Before we leave, Von lists all of our duties on her clipboard. "Hustle out," she tells us, "and look like you having a serious good time." She even color-coordinates us—navy for the first round play, turquoise if we get into the quarterfinals, baby blue for the semis, and bright sunflower yellow for the finals. We're coordinated down to our shoes and shoelaces.

My grandma and Uncle Charlie drop us off at the Hilo Airport. "Howzit, Charlie," Coach Huggie says, and they shake hands, macho-style. "This girl of yours is the best thing that ever happened to my team."

"I thought I was," Coach Kaaina says.

"Erma, you still gorgeous as ever," Uncle Charlie says as he plants one on her cheek.

"Charlie, better you leave your girl to us already." She places both hands firmly on Von's shoulders. "Let her live my house. She so organized, it's unbelievable. And once softball season start, I going adopt her."

Von looks like she feeling pretty good about herself, until Uncle Charlie says, "And to think, this kid of mine half-stupid like me. Pocho-power," he says, raising a clenched fist in the air. Von looks so sharp in her navy blazer with khaki pants till Uncle says that.

"You so stupid, Charlie," Grandma tells him. "Yvonne, tell your mother what nonsense he talking and she shut him up fast. No better yet, I tell her for you, okay?" Von smiles a crooked half-grin.

Then Sterling comes out from the crowd of boys and family. Genevieve's hanging on to his sleeve.

She had told him about what happened with Kyle in hopes of turning him against me. So Sterling called Von. Then Von called me. Then we conference-called. Von, Sterling, and I talked for hours and hours about it. After we all hung up, I more fully understood what was *not* said among us—the lies built on the untold lies:

I continued writing Kyle's papers to keep the peace, but I said nothing.

Sterling really wanted a scholarship. He needed Kyle, but said nothing of this.

Von was still with Babes, Kyle's cousin. And she

never confronted them again about what he did to me at Wailoa.

"Hi, Mr. Vierra, Mrs. Kaya," Sterling says as he shakes hands with Uncle and kisses Grandma. "I be watching out for these two so that no Honolulu boys, nobody, get close to them."

"Never mind them," Uncle Charlie tells Sterling, "just set and serve like you did all season. And kick these two girls' butts if they get in the way." Viva laughs, then folds her arms and looks the other way. "Emi-lou and Yvonne, you stay out of the boys' way. You just a couple of freshmen going along for the ride." Viva nods in agreement.

I don't know why Uncle Charlie likes to put us in our place in front of the very people who want to see us humiliated. Sterling puts his big arms around Von and me and says, "I still be watching out for them. Get plenty Honolulu townie sharks on the hunt for sweet okole."

"Sterling!" Coach Kaaina scolds and everybody laughs. "Well, we better hele-on."

Sterling follows her holding Von and me. I turn around, all crushed in his arms, to wave bye to Grandma, who has that sad look of airport good-byes on her face like I'm never coming back.

"I see you in a few days, Grandma," I tell her.

Sterling sits with the boys on the flight over. Babes sits by the window, Von next to her, and Viva on the aisle seat. I sit across the aisle from them by myself.

I didn't figure on all of us girls sleeping together until the moment Von turns the key to the room at the

Pagoda Hotel. I stare at the two double beds.

Babes and Von quickly put their bags on one of the beds and Viva put hers on the other one. "I call the desk for one cot, Louie," Viva snaps. "'Cause hell if I like sleep next to you."

"Ditto, dammit," I mutter.

"Nah, maybe I sneak out and sleep with Sterling," Viva adds, "and if I no get caught, you can have the bed." Only Babes laughs.

"And what make you think he like you, Viva?" Von asks. "If you ask me, you dreaming this whole thing, what you think, Babes?"

Babes smirks and shrugs her shoulders. "Maybe, maybe not."

"Not acording to Kyle, right, Babes?" Viva answers. "Kyle said, 'The boy keeping his options open.'"

"That's what I heard," Babes adds. "I told you that," she says, nudging Von.

I shoot a look at Von.

"And Louie–kinda looking chunky, eh?" Viva laughs. "Ten more pounds and Sterling be too shame to be seen with Emi-fat, eat a rat with dark roots in need of another tint." She and Babes high-five each other.

"All that makeup and lip gloss don't hide your true colors either," I say softly.

"What, Emi-lou? Speak up," Viva challenges me.

I sit on a small chair.

"You did us a favor telling Sterling about what happened to Louie at Wailoa," Von says. "He know everything that went on that night, and he still like Louie.

No need lie to him no more. Louie and me told him everything."

"Just friends, right? Or small-kine more than friends? What exactly that mean?" Viva asks.

"So many rumors, so little time," Babes muses.

"And if you told Sterling everything," Viva says, "then why didn't he kick Kyle's ass? I mean, if he care for her so much, you would think he would do something, right?" she snipes as she points her chin at me.

Von looks at me. "Because," she says. "Be-cuz. It's a family thing." Babes give Von a half smile.

Somebody knocks on the door. "Coach says we get till dinnertime to cruise," Sterling tells us. "No games till tomorrow at ten, Iolani gym. Louie, my cousin Chadwick said he picking us up in front the hotel to go Ala Moana, if you like."

"Ho, I like come, Sterling," Viva begs in a baby voice.

"And what," Von says, "be the third wheel, cho-chin, carrying the lantern ten feet behind the first wife? Sheez, Ala Moana right there, we go walk, Viva. Me, you, and Babes. See you guys dinnertime and no be late, Louie, 'cause I no like Mr. Teixeira think I cannot handle my crew. I mean it, okay?"

I nod to Von. "C'mon, Louie," Sterling says, "there his red Honda. Check you laters, Von."

Sterling makes me sit in the front with his cousin Chadwick and he climbs in the back. "Eh, Cuz, whas-sup?" Sterling says. "This my–friend–Louie." Sterling reaches around the seat and holds me. "You my–friend, right?"

167

"You tenth grade, same with my cuz?" Chadwick asks. "You get friends or what, I mean for me?"

Sterling laughs, then says, "We give him Viva, Louie. They match. She like your type, brah."

"No way," I tell him. "She like Sterling and she cute but–"

"Why, why, she one dog or something? How you know she like my type? Eh, Cuz, what's my type? I no like no hounds from Hilo. What, she ugs or what? Nah, no answer that–I take um back. I no like nobody. I get my own chick."

"Nah, we fix you up," Sterling teases.

"She gotta be ugs," Chadwick grumbles, "or what, one Klingon, or what, Arnold Ziffle? Change the subject already. You guys like go cruising little while? What Grandma and Grandpa told you, Sterling? What time you guys gotta be back?"

"Six," I tell him.

"And Grandma said you have to eat dinner with us tonight," Sterling says, punching his cousin's arm.

"Shoots, brah. Beat my mother's cooking. Us had Portagee bean soup for the last three nights, brah. Ho, yes, Grams and Gramps, here comes your gassy grandson to grind some steaks and lobsters, look out."

Chadwick takes us up Tantalus, down Daimond Head, through Waikīkī down Kuhio Avenue, and around Magic Island. "So what, like go Ala Moana?" he asks.

Real fast, Sterling answers, "Yeah, brah, I like buy some stuffs. Park by Town and Country, Chadwick."

Sterling holds my hand as we cross the street. He

buys a T-shirt for himself and me, the same kind, and he makes me choose one for my grandma for golf, from him. Then we walk to the 14-Carat Plum. Sterling buys me a turquoise silver ring for my baby finger. His grandma and mother gave him lots of spending money. I had some money from Grandma and Uncle Charlie, so I buy for Sterling a silver chain with a cursive *S* charm and he buys me one with cursive *E* and *L* charms.

"Oh, how cute you country hicks are—buying initials for each other. *So sweet.*" Chadwick clasps his hands together over his heart. "I gotta remember this one for when I like score, too."

"Eh, good idea, cuz, I wear Louie's and she wear mine, okay, Louie? See Chadwick, you smart for something, too—sometimes." Chadwick rolls his eyes and pretends to play the violin with his two fingers as Sterling bends down to put his chain around my neck. He moves my hair and his lips brush the base of my neck.

I climb into the backseat of the car and put my chain around Sterling's neck when he sits down in the front. I wrap my arms around him. This is how it must feel to have a boyfriend. A little more than a boy who is a friend, like Rudy and me—but then again, we're more like two girlfriends.

I think about Von backing me up in the hotel room. These good feelings move inside me like waves; they make the whole sleeping arrangement at the hotel seem kind of all right. We head back to the Pagoda for dinner.

38.
Messed Up

Von imposes a lights-out at nine o'clock policy. Never mind what the boys are doing. According to Von, the boys are Coach Huggie's problems. "We ain't going be part of any hassles," she reminds us. We all crash out–two of them on one bed, Viva on hers, and me on the cot.

The boys do really well the next morning. In their first match, they wipe out the Castle Knights. I like the feeling of having somebody who's a boyfriend-like in the game. Sterling sits next to me on my end of the bench and puts his chain in my hand. "Wear um for me till the game pau," he says.

Viva gets so mad, Von takes her to the scoreboard table. "I going kick her ass, she wait, fat imitation nobody copycat." She tugs at her tight dress and clunks over to the table in her high heels.

"She acting like she get something going with him," I whisper to Von when she comes back to the bench. She shrugs her shoulders and shakes her head. Then she motions for me to pay attention to the game.

That same afternoon, the boys play their quarter-final game against the Kaimukī Bulldogs. It's rough playing two matches in one day. The boys look tired, the Kaainas screaming at them for lousy passes. Sterling can't seem to set the wide and low passes.

Von works with me on stats, so I don't mess up and get yelled at, too. They go into three games and the last two we win 17–15 and 15–13.

Coach Kaaina's pissed. On the bus back to the Pagoda, she yells, "I ain't kidding, that was one match we should've lost. Kyle, you not covering on the rotation and they catching you on the weak side all the time. Levi making big man with the big gun. And what, Baron, trying to get Coach Cannon notice you for the UH Rainbows? Knock off the scholarship hot-dogging, man. And Sterling, none of that fancy setting crap, you hear me, son? Basics, dammit."

"And I tell you all something," Coach Huggie adds, "curfew is nine o'clock, you hear me? I want you all to sleep well."

"Some of you boys think this is a party, sneaking in and out of your rooms and doing the devil," Coach Kaaina says. "I raised four sons, two daughters, and now this one here," she says, pointing to Sterling. "I ain't here for my health. I here to win, you hear me? And you can resume your dirty habits once we back in Hilo for all I care. But with me, I want your minds clear—no dope, no nothing, or you will be sorry you ever crossed my path."

Coach Huggie tightens his lips and nods his head the

whole time. "No substances, boys," Mr. Teixeira says. "School regulations are in effect here, too."

It's about seven-thirty when we come back from dinner. We're all on the same floor and our room's way down the hall past the Kaaina's and even past Mr. Teixeira's room. The boys all leave their doors open. Everybody's relaxing as Von, Babes, and I trudge down the hall.

Viva's in Kyle and Sterling's room. She's lying on Kyle's bed. Levi, Baron, and Spencer hang out there, too. When we walk past, Sterling gets up and runs after us. "Wagging his tongue at that little kid, wasting his time," Kyle says. "I swear, Sterling, you acting stupider than stupid." Viva laughs the loudest.

When we get to our room, Von and Babes lie down on their bed and turn on the TV. Sterling pulls me by the bathroom. I feel his body press close to mine. He places his finger like a gun in my gut and jokes, "Gimme back my *E* and *L*, right now, Louie."

He walks into the room and wedges himself between Von and Babes. "Von, you better go right now and get Viva out of my room," he says, "'cause they drinking– even after what my grandma said. That's up to them, but what get me is that we can take states." Sterling pauses. "But they so messed up, man."

"You guys can win," I tell him.

"Thank you, Rebecca of Sunnybrook Farm," Babes mutters. "But some guys only here to par-tay."

"Eh, Kyle getting Viva drunk," Sterling whispers to Von, "and plan is, you know, he like–"

Von jumps up from her bed, walks out the door, and

slams it behind her. Babes follows and watches from our doorway. Pretty soon Viva's getting arm-dragged and pushed down the hall. When she walks past, she smells like my mother.

Von doesn't want us to get screwed, too. She puts Viva in her bed, turns off the TV and the lights, and says, "Just go, Sterling. I don't want Coach even bed-check us. If the lights out, she ain't coming inside. She just count heads from the door. Stupid Kyle. Go, hurry up."

Viva's crying on her bed.

"Stupid, you Viva. He was going use you," Von says to her.

"Check you guys later," Sterling says. "Louie-Louie, you sleep good. Wear your yellow dress tomorrow—you right, watch, we going win states."

39.
The Truth Be Told

The team plays their semifinal game against second-seed Kamehameha. The match goes three games, but we win. That night is the finals—against the Punahou Buff-and-Blue. They won states ten years in a row already, but the buzz is that Hilo can take them this year. An outer-island team rarely takes states.

The coaches want the team back at the hotel to rest and relax, no monkey business. Viva goes down to the pool with Kyle and Levi. Von, Babes, and I drink sodas and watch TV.

Sterling comes to our room. He sits on my cot and tells me something that makes no sense in my ear just to breathe heavy and tickle me. Fooling around with him makes me feel uneasy ever since Roxanne came home. How much am I really like her?

All of a sudden, Babes asks, "You guys *going* or what?" She says this like she's disgusted. "I mean, so what, Sterling, I thought you was checking out Viva. What, you no like her? You blind or you just stupid, or what? I mean, Viva is Miss Everything, and Louie—she just dragging your rep down."

Von nudges her with her elbow. "No," she says to Von, "I close with Viva. This damn Louie is a Xerox copy of her. Open your eye, Sterling. And no be acting all lovey-dovey in front of me, okay? You making me sick."

Von doesn't say a word.

"Then beat it," I tell her.

"What?" Babes says. "You think I forgot what you did in the bathroom, hah? You like me kick your ass again? Tell her the truth, Von."

"Von no need tell me nothing," I tell Babes. "She trying hard to keep peace between all us."

She laughs. "Tell her, Von. Tell her what you and Sterling been cooking up behind her back. I no care what you say, Von, I cannot stand her and I cannot stand that you still friends with her. Eh, truth be told, right?"

"Eh, Von," Sterling says nervously, "take care your animal. No be lipping off, Babes, you ugly, fat—" Sterling stops himself.

"The truth be told," Babes says looking at Von. "He was only baby-sitting for us, right, Von?"

"What?" I look at Von and Sterling.

"That's not true," Sterling says grabbing on to my arm. "That's how this started. But that's not how it is now, I promise, Louie."

I turn to Von. "Baby-sitting?" She looks away from me.

"I sorry, Louie," Sterling says. "Von, tell her that ain't how it is now."

"Sorry?" I tell him.

"Louie," Von says, "No blame him. Babes and me, we–"

"You what? Tell me." I glare at Babes.

"What? What you looking at, hah, Louie?" Babes yells at me. "She the one, Von, making all the trouble between us. Now Viva all pissed at me, too. And Sterling use to be close with Kyle, until this troublemaking bitch came along."

"I never did nothing to you, Babes," I mutter. "I even been trying to–"

"Yeah, right, you never did nothing. You the biggest troublemaker I know. Playing all your stupid mind games with me and Von. And the worst part is, you look so damn innocent while you do it. You never even gave me a chance."

"I tried," I tell Babes. "She the one ain't trying," I say to Von, who tightens her jaw.

"Try harder," Babes says. Then she glares at me. "I ain't pau with you yet."

"The bus leaving," Levi calls into our room, "C'mon, hurry up."

"I pau with all of you," I say as I walk out of the room.

40.
Nobody

Hilo takes the first game and Punahou takes the next. I don't know what happened in the deciding game. Sometimes, when you're from Hilo, you think you're nobody next to private school, rich Honolulu townies—so even if you can win, you end up losing.

Kyle mistimes a couple of crucial blocks that turn the game around. Levi, probably tired from drinking the night before and from the game earlier that day, hits the ball on the tape two or three times. And Sterling, for some reason, starts calling the wrong patterns. One time, he back-sets the ball and nobody's there. Some spectators laugh at him.

Coach Huggie jumps off the bench and yells, "Time out!"

"What you guys doing?" he yells at the boys. "Just keep the ball in play." Sterling looks confused. I know he feels the game slipping away like it's all his fault. "Sterling, you listening to me? I want the ball to go to Kyle, you hear me, son? Set Kyle."

Game ball for Punahou. Hilo wants the side out. The serve goes deep and Levi passes it close to the net, so close that Sterling never has a chance to make a decent play. Net violation. Game, set, match. State title to Punahou.

Sterling hangs his towel over his head on the bench. I come over and drape his warm-up over his shoulders. "Was all my fault," he says. "I messed us up." He doesn't even look at me.

Later on, Sterling comes out of the locker room, but he walks onto the bus with the boys. Then Chadwick arrives at the Pagoda Hotel and goes into Sterling's room.

I feel so bad for him that I let the whole baby-sitting thing momentarily pass. I want him to come and talk to me. That's how it goes in the movies. The woman comforts the man. But Von tells me, "Leave him alone. I no think he like us there, know what I mean? He like handle this himself."

"How you know, Von?" I ask her.

"Sterling told me. So Louie, nothing, no worry. Just kick back, know what I mean? Whoa, Louie-Louie, this is deeper than the deep blue sea," she says to me. "Let him find his way. He be all right."

She's being nice to me. It's my moment to grill her. "You better tell me the baby-sitting deal, Von."

"Later," she says, brushing me off and looking in the crowd of people for Babes. "No worry."

"And you never talk to me about Roxanne's options," I tell her. "The time I called you before the trip but you was going Longs with her." Von's eyes continue searching. "Tell me why my mother chose none of the above?"

"What, Louie? You talking bubbles. Babes, wait," she calls.

"Oh, never mind." I feel disappointment sink in.

Once back at the hotel, we're tired so the lights go out. I'm wondering why Viva listened to Von about leaving the boys alone. She didn't question her or raise a fuss. I can't sleep. The baby-sitting's on my mind. Yet I feel all wrapped up with Sterling and the necklaces, T-shirts, and the turquoise ring that I keep twirling on my finger. I pay no mind to Von and Babes in the same bed, under the same cover, or to Viva, who's obviously awake.

Someone knocks lightly at the door and Viva jumps out of bed to answer. At first I think it's Sterling, but when I look from the corner of my eye, it's Kyle. He climbs into bed with Viva.

I can't believe it. I pretend to be asleep even when he gets up and peers into my face. I hear sheets pulling, and limbs moving under the covers. I try to remain still so they think I'm asleep.

The room is pitch-black. The air conditioner hums loudly. I don't know who's making out with whom. Is it Kyle and Viva? Or is it Von and Babes? Both couples? Can't be. Von wouldn't be so inconsiderate. No way.

I should've used the bathroom before getting into bed. How long will I be trapped here in this position? I could slide off the cot and leave the room. I can't. The sounds intensify.

And then I smell Kyle's cologne, the way I tasted it in

my mouth the night he tried to–I start feeling a cold sweat and the rising of a dry heave. I remember how they all came to help me. Von taking care of me.

But tonight, I'm here, alone. A nobody. Nothing. I turn slightly and see Babes with her arms around Von from behind. The dark room closes in on me.

I let the tears slide down my face and remain motionless. I feel so uncomfortable, like watching a sex scene on HBO with my grandma in the room. I'm participating against my will. It's so unfair. Stupid little nobody, all by myself, and Genevieve giggling under the sheets.

41.
Half-Truths

"Eh, why you so grumpy, Louie?" Von asks. "The whole flight home, all morning, you never said nothing to me." Babes nudges her from behind as they disembark the plane.

Von turns around. "C'mon, Louie, hurry up. You all right? You sleep good last night? You look tired."

"What you think?" I mutter in the jetway. I fumble with my carry-on bags. Tourists, families, the whole volleyball team passes me by.

"C'mon," Von says.

"What's her trip?" Babes asks. She takes Von's arm and they get on the escalator.

"You better wait for me, Yvonne," I tell her.

"Well, step it up," Von says. "I waiting, jeez, Louie." She pushes through the crowd near the baggage claim area.

I struggle with my bags to keep up with her. Sterling tries to take one from me. "And where you was last night?" I ask him.

"Whoa, stand back from the possessive-chick types all the time, Jardine," Kyle tells him.

Sterling puts his hand on my hair. "Get away," I tell him. "Von, wait for me."

"Go get our bags, son," Coach Kaaina tells Sterling, "right now." She gives me a dirty look.

I see Babe's father putting Von's bags in their truck. Kyle hops in back. They pull away from the curb.

"What's going on?" Grandma asks. "I was suppose to take Yvonne home. Hey now, how come you so sad?" She presses my face between her hands. We walk toward the car.

It's everything that I'd kept from her, all the secrets and half-truths, now tantamount to lies.

I never mentioned a word about missing and needing Roxanne because I wanted to seem strong inside, I could take it, I was tough just like Grandma.

I said nothing about taking all those diet pills, laxatives, and diuretics that Von had been shoplifting for months.

I told her half-truths about Sterling, pretending we were just friends in front of her, but kissing and touching him outside.

I never told her what I knew about Von and Babes, what I had seen them doing in the bathroom, the way they looked at each other, and the way they played and laughed with each other.

I never told her about what happened with Kyle at Wailoa.

When we get into the car in the hot parking lot, I feel it all in my chest, rising and writhing. "Emi-lou, talk to me." Grandma hands me a Kleenex.

"I dunno where to start," I whisper.

"Start where it hurt the most," she says, putting her hand on my knee.

"Grandma, you know something–Von, she one, she one–" I stutter.

"Lesbian."

I look at my grandma's face and see no change to anger or shock or disappointment.

"What happened, Emi-lou?" She looks me right in the eye. "You her femme, Emi-lou?" I know Grandma learned this from Aunty Vicky. "And who gave you that ring? Yvonne? And that chain–what's that?"

"I not," I tell her, "Von is." I hadn't meant to tell her about Von. I wanted to tell her what went on in the room. No names. No real details. Just hint at it to get it off my chest.

"Well?" Grandma asks. "Who gave you the jewelry?"

"She was doing something with Babes at the hotel room," I blurt out. "And that's not all. Remember the time Babes gave me lickings? Was 'cause I busted in on their stall at school."

"Bust in their stall?" Grandma asks. "Emi-lou, you better start telling me what's going on, the whole story."

I hesitate. What am I getting myself into? I start to feel light, my breathing shallow. But as I talk to her, everything begins to fall off my shoulders. So I tell her all about the stalls in A-building bathroom and the hickey Von got from Babes. I tell Grandma about the Halloween Dance. I'm the world's biggest squealer. And I'm the world's biggest liar.

Some part of me knows that the more I tell her about

Von, the more she won't know about me. But as I tell Grandma these stories, I realize that neither of us can stop Von from being with Babes.

Grandma rolls down all the windows. "Emi-lou," she says, "I going tell you something I learn from being old like I am. Far as I concern, Yvonne is who she is. You cannot change that. She was born the way she is."

"Hah? You saying she cannot change?" Her response is so unexpected.

"Nope, and the best thing for you to do is to stop trying to make her be like you. She ain't and never will be. You the best friends that ever was—and I tell you, come as a relief that you ain't her girlfriend—I cannot lie to you, Emi-lou, 'cause that cross my mind many a time. And if you guys was together in that way—what would I tell Charlie?"

"And what if we was, Grandma?" I ask her.

"That's what I trying to tell you, Emi-lou. Even if you was lesbian, celibate, promiscuous, super-religious, atheist, vegetarian, save the rain forest, save the whales—in the end, you would still be mine, 'cause you one Kaya. Get what I saying? Love is love. You receive it in whatever form it arrives in."

"Grandma, you cannot tell nobody, okay? Please." I feel the tears rising, so I breathe deeply. I rest my face on Grandma's shoulder.

"Some part of me know I screwed up my own daughters, Emi-lou," she says. "Not that I agree with everything you might choose, but I not going let my old-fashioned attitudes mess you up."

She says nothing for a long time. Then she takes a

deep breath. "Emi-lou—Etsuko, Charlie, and me been friends long before you girls was born. We known each other since high school days, and your grandpa was Charlie's best man. But I with you on this one. I promise you. I not saying nothing."

I hold her even tighter. "Grandma, you saying that— to you, that's all right if Von is like that? Sterling sort of told me the same thing."

Grandma breaks in. "Oh, so that's who that *S* is on your chain? You will be telling me all about that when you ready, right?"

I nod.

"I have to trust you, Emi-lou."

I stare at my hands. I want to tell her that I feel like Roxanne when I'm with Sterling, but I don't say anything. My silence makes me a liar.

"But one thing at a time." Grandma pats my head. "Best you think open-minded. Best you and me be there for Yvonne, no matter what—'cause we would want Yvonne do the same for us, right?"

We pull out of the airport and stop to pick up cigarettes from Kai Store on the way home. Grandma's having her one before-dinner cigarette, the smoke slipping out of the crack in the window like ghost fingers rushing out into the night.

42.
Damn Dyke

On a Friday night at Wailoa, a drunk Viva tells Aunty Vicky everything that went on in our room at the Pagoda Hotel. It's Saturday when Aunty Ets, Aunty Vicky, Grandma, and I play the back nine at the Hilo Municipal. By the time we hit the 19th Hole Bar and Grill, Aunty Etsuko is on the phone with Uncle Charlie.

"What's going on?" Grandma says as she sits down with her Coke. Aunty Vicky shrugs. "Who she talking to for so long? You rode with Aunty Ets. What happened? She look upset. Vicky, what you said to her?"

"So you just assume it's me?" Aunty Vicky says, lighting a cigarette. "Why no ask Louie? She was there."

Grandma and I look at each other.

"You big mouth," I say as I take a swing at my aunty. She pushes me away. "What you said about Von?"

"Stop it," Grandma tells me. Aunty Ets sits down. "Go get Aunty Ets a Seven Up," she tells me.

"Charlie's on his way down. Emi-lou," she says,

stopping me with her hand, "why did I have to hear this from Vicky? Why didn't you say something?"

"I, we," I stammer.

"She told me, Ets," Grandma says. "She told me everything. I promised Emi-lou that I wouldn't–"

"Why, Lea?" Aunty Ets asks. "Wouldn't you want me to tell you if any of your girls were getting into this kind of trouble. Yvonne's in over her head."

"Trouble?" Grandma asks. "And how we would stop them? We just push them farther and farther away from us."

I see Uncle Charlie's car enter the parking lot. He walks toward our table with a deliberate anger in his step. "How long you known this, Emi-lou?" he asks. "Goddammit, why didn't you tell us sooner? What's the matter with you? Half-stupid too, huh? You kids make me sick. I don't know how the hell I was trusting you all this time, when you just a couple of good-for-nothing, wanna-be butchies."

I put my hands over my ears. I want to scream.

"And don't you ever, ever call her Von again, you hear me, Emi-lou? Her name is Yvonne. Yvonne Vierra, name after my own mother. Sheez, imagine that, Ets, our only daughter. Make me sick, I tell you."

"Charlie, you better knock it off," Grandma warns. She looks around and speaks in hushed tones. "And don't you dare blame Emi-lou. Wasn't easy for her to tell and not easy for her to accept. I best be telling you, Charlie, that you think this one over good. Yvonne's your only kid, and what, you want to turn her away from you now? You no think she little bit confuse, too?"

Aunty Etsuko starts crying. She puts her face in her hands. "You're too late, Leatrice," she says, "it's all too late."

"What?" Grandma asks. "What happened?"

"Charlie made Yvonne call Kris already, didn't you, Charlie? And he forced her to end their friendship."

"Friendship?" Uncle Charlie yells. "Vicky, tell them. They butchie lovers, right?"

She nods.

"They are," I whisper, "friends."

"You don't know nothing about friendship. Shut your mouth," he tells me.

"You don't know nothing about love," Grandma says.

"Love?" Uncle Charlie laughs. "Gimme a break, Lea."

"Do you know how humiliating it was for Yvonne to call Kris right in front to you? Do you, Charlie?" Aunty Ets asks.

"Oh, no, Charlie," Grandma gasps as she puts her forehead in her hand. She doesn't look up for a long time.

"And that's not all, Leatrice. He said he's sending her to see a therapist." Aunty Etsuko cries some more and wipes her face with cocktail napkins. "What am I going to do about this man, Leatrice?" she says pointing an accusing finger at Uncle Charlie. "You didn't even give us time to think about our options."

That word again. I feel like eating a boatful of fries, a chili dog with lots of cheese, everything sweet.

"You knock it off, you hear me, Etsuko," Uncle Charlie says softly. "I told you the day I met you. I had ten brothers and sisters and I wanted none of it in my life. I one old man and I get this kid doing who-knows-what. I told you, Etsuko."

Grandma puts her arm around Aunty Ets. She head-jerks me to get out of earshot. I run toward the Pro Shop, then pause by the door. I hear my grandma scold Uncle Charlie.

"Yvonne is who she is, you ain't changing that—both of you. No matter what we do, our kids get their own spirit and they make their own choices."

I sit outside the Pro Shop and press my back into the wall.

"Look, my kids, they ain't perfect. Roxanne, I hate to say this, but she still don't know who or what she is. And Vicky—jeez, she on the ten-year college plan. My Amy—sad to say but that one think she so high and mighty, might as well be haole already. But I love them all. And I tell you something, I lucky if Emi-lou ain't the most messed up with all that happen to her already. Think twice, Charlie. Yvonne's a good kid with plenty talents. No throw nothing away."

"Yeah, well, she ain't going out for softball this summer. And Erma and Huggie ain't having her suit up this year either. Forget that."

"Charlie!" Aunty Etsuko gets up. "We better listen to Leatrice, you hear me, Charlie? I'm going home to talk to Yvonne. Coming, Charlie?"

Uncle Charlie storms past me. He stops, then turns to face me. "I trusted you," he says, poking his finger in my chest. "When Yvonne see that doctor, you going with her. Maybe we save you from being a damn dyke."

Grandma reaches for my hand. "You did the right thing," she whispers. "Wait till we get home. Vicky's ass is grass."

"I ain't a dyke," I tell my grandma.

"What?"

"Maybe I more like Roxanne."

"What?" Grandma asks again. This time she stops in the middle of the parking lot. "How you like *her*?"

"A mess by fourteen." And then we are silent.

43.
Detention

Von hasn't talked to me all week since we came back from Honolulu. This morning, she comes to school real late. First recess, she doesn't wait for me. She goes straight to A-building bathroom. The v.p., Mr. Chong, calls Von from her Period Four class. I see her leaving from the next room with a pink office pass.

At lunch recess, I see Von by the office with a putty knife scraping gum off of the sidewalk. I head up to the high school campus when Mr. Chong stops me. He says, "Hang on there, Emi-lou. Yvonne tells me that you also hang out at the A-building bathroom during recess. Well, that's all over now. You are off-limits—the high school campus is a restricted area. No intermediate students are to loiter there during recess. Do you hear me? Here's your putty knife. You're on detention with Yvonne for breaking school rules. And your tardies are astronomical."

I cannot believe it. I feel numb. Where do I go if I cannot hang out at A-building bathroom? Rudy went and joined every club and I didn't tag along. I had Sterling and Von. I know Rudy wouldn't get mad at me if I decided to follow him, but I know I would feel uncomfortable with some of his new friends.

When lunch recess ends, Von doesn't come to our P.E. class. She cuts out and probably heads up to A-building bathroom. Period Six, I go to my newswriting class; Sterling walks in tardy. He calls me to the back of the room.

"I was with Von and Babes all last period," Sterling says. He pulls my chair close to his. "Why you told your grandma, Louie? Remember when the three of us promised not to say anything? Von and me was going take care of things? She never told. How come you told? She pissed. Babes is super-pissed. And she going use this all the way to make Von turn against you, Louie."

I'm so sick of this. They're all blaming me. "Viva told my aunty Vicky," I tell him. "That's how they found out."

"But Von stay mad 'cause you told your grandma, end of story, you broke the promise us all made." He looks at me then pushes his chair away from the desk.

"And where you was on the night you guys lost to Punahou?" I ask him. "You was in your room smoking with your cousin Chadwick. Where was Kyle? You even notice that he was gone? He was in our room with Viva, and I hope Von told you what she was doing with Babes. And all while I was in the room."

Sterling hits the wall with his fist. "But you still should've never told. Her father called the school to report this. And she seeing the damn school psychologist and her counselor, too. Louie, remember, I told you—"

"I remember. I was confuse. I was scared. I didn't mean for all this to happen."

"Von and me close, you know that, right, Louie? We all going work it out—today, A-building bathroom, after school."

Kyle starts inching closer to us. "What you guys talking about? No, no need tell me, I know."

"You don't know nothing," I tell him.

"I feel sorry for you, Emi-lou. You trying so hard to be bad like the rest of the girls." Kyle laughs.

"What you talking about?" Sterling asks.

"This," he says pointing his chin at me, "this small kid. No let her come between all us, Jardine." Kyle puts his hands on Sterling's shoulders. "We got athletic scholarships in our future and all Klingon chicks do is screw things up."

"We, me and Louie, we—" Sterling stutters as he looks around, the rest of the class gathering around us now. "We just friends."

"Right," Kyle tells him.

I feel so embarrassed. "See," Sissy Miyamoto whispers to Jenni Takitani, "Genevieve told me the same thing. They're *just friends.*"

I look at Sterling. "Louie," he starts.

"Some friend she is," Kyle says about me. "Bigmouth, wanna-be dork. I wanted to win states so bad—but you had your mind on other things."

"You blaming me for losing states?" Sterling asks.

"Nah, not even, 'cause we get next year, Jardine. But

brah, you gotta cut her loose. She trouble with a big T."

"Even after what you did to me down Wailoa–" I start. "And Von telling me you Babe's cuz, so let it go for her sake–"

"You can believe that, brah?" Sterling cuts in. "We was going let that slide." He shoves Kyle hard. They start pushing and shoving until the campus security pulls them apart and escorts both of them to the office.

44.
Ex-Best

After school, I wait for Sterling by A-building bathroom. He walks away from the office and lights a cigarette. He sits down next to me. "Suspended," he says. "Three days."

"Shucks, who going baby-sit me?" I ask him.

"Eh, Louie," he says, "if you don't know by now—"

"What?" I ask him. "We just friends, right?"

Before he answers, Von and Babes arrive. "She sorry, man, what can she say?" he starts.

"She can tell us sorry from her own big mouth," Babes says from between gritted teeth. "Von's parents not going know we still hanging out as friends, right? Unless her ex-best friend tell them. And tell you what, Von could use a few trustworthy friends right now."

"Viva told Aunty Vicky," I say to Von. She looks at me for a moment. "And I made one mistake. I told my grandma, but she promise to never say anything to—"

Von's face hardens. She shakes her head. "See,"

Babes sneers, "she told, the end, all pau. You history, Louie."

"Eh, Babes, you promise me this wouldn't get ugly."

"Ugly? Eh, like talk ugly, talk to her," she says jabbing her finger in my chest. "How you like me tell her grandma that you been doing Louie here? And the worse part, that's all lies. We wasn't doing nothing in that hotel room."

"I not lying," I tell Von. "How I lying?" Von looks the other way. I'm trying not to look scared, even if I'm afraid of Babes.

Babes laughs. "Von, I told you—Emi-lou's a big time, pain-in-the-ass troublemaker. I told you, right?"

Von shrugs, then nods. "I thought we could all get along," she says.

"Why you backing her up?" I ask Von.

"You never even gave Babes a chance."

"Three's a crowd," I tell her.

"Shut up, Louie," Von says. "So much for your lies to me at Leleiwi. You can accept, right? I doubt it."

"I did," I tell her, "accept. But why you had to shove it in my face in the hotel room?"

There's a long, dead silence.

"So what, Von?" Sterling asks at last. She looks at Babes first, then she averts her eyes from mine.

"Sorry might sound good to me. I never told anybody about Kyle. A promise is a promise, right, Sterling?" Von says, mean. He doesn't respond. "Whatevers, man. But I ain't going feel for Louie what I did before."

"You never told," I yell at her, "because they would blame *you*. How come you wasn't watching out for me?

'Cause you was making out with Babes in her truck, that's why. And my aunty Vicky was stoned. We all liars."

Sterling gets between us.

Babes lights a cigarette and another one for Von. Von drags deeply. She looks at me and smirks a disgusted laugh. She passes her cigarette to Sterling and he takes a deep drag. The smoke hangs around Von's face. She follows Babes down the long sidewalk to the parking lot across the street. And Von never looks back.

Her words kill me all the way inside.

I ain't going feel for Louie what I did before.

45.
Missing Von

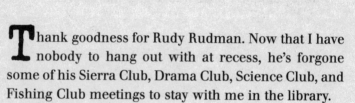

Thank goodness for Rudy Rudman. Now that I have nobody to hang out with at recess, he's forgone some of his Sierra Club, Drama Club, Science Club, and Fishing Club meetings to stay with me in the library.

"You think I using you, Rudy?" I ask him.

"You are, honey-boom," he replies, "but you make up for it eventually with your volunteerism in all my student gov committees and your fabulous makeup collection hawked by Von. Oops."

"No mention her name," I remind him.

"Sorry," he whispers. "Besides, Uncle Rudy loves our on-again, off-again romance. Lover can't be glued to your side for days with his social schedule, dahling."

"I deep in like with you, Rudy."

He kisses my hand then looks around. "Can't be letting my suitors see my infidelities." He laughs. "You seen Von around?"

"No, but Sterling said he call her almost every night," I tell him.

"You not jealous or nothing?" Rudy asks as he pops a stick of illegal gum in his mouth. "C'mon, truth be told."

"No chew gum," I scold. "Where we going hang out if we get kick out of here?"

"No worry," he says, "we can hang out at the student gov room and shag this bad excuse of a room with butt-smelling air-conditioning. So what Von said to him?" he asks.

"Not much," I tell him, "but he my only link to Von. She no even come to poker night anymore. Sterling said she no tell him nothing deep like she use to. She think he going tell me."

"Wow, you no hate that, girlfriend?"

"At least she still talking."

"True, Louie, so true," Rudy says patting my hand. "I seen Von all over the place with Babes, you know, Louie."

"Where? They look happy?" I ask him. "I mean, Von—she look happy without me?"

"What you think, girlfriend? Girlfriend has a girl-friend. They cruising down the beach in that truck, at the mall, basketball games, you name it, girl—where Uncle Rudy been, he seen the couple of the year in all their glory. I thought her father said yikes to the dykes."

"Yeah, I know," I tell him. "She not suppose to be with Babes, not even as friends. I guess she going behind their back." I feel so sad. "She keep getting farther and farther away from me. Maybe I really should've accept Babes. You remember that day at Leleiwi?"

"No, I was sunning my buff bod, remember?'

"I told Von I could deal with what's-her-face."

"Kris. Babes. Whatever. Would help, you know. To accept, all the way, down to the bone, to the core, the bottom of your heart—"

"I get it," I tell him. The bell rings. I stand up and pull Rudy's arm so he gets going to class. "So you coming with me to the doubleheader tonight against Laupāhoehoe?"

"Sterling asked me if I wanted to go," I tell him.

"C'mon, Louie, we go."

"Okay, okay," I tell him, but I really don't want to go. I know that Viva's there, still after Sterling, but I'd rather not be there. So much for being possessive. And Babes hates me bad. And Von. I miss Von so bad, I feel this all the way inside.

46.
Nothing to Me

Von makes the high school varsity team. But Uncle Charlie and Aunty Ets go to every game and every practice to supervise her.

The field glows green neon and the lights buzz orange white. At night, the field looks shiny and wet grass cuttings stick to my feet. Rudy sits in the dugout with Anita and Rae. He's on stats. He gives me little finger waves every now and then.

When Sterling and I take our seats on the bleachers near the dugout, Von turns her face to us, then looks the other way. I don't know how or why Sterling takes all of this. Some part of me thinks he can handle it all. Another part of me knows he can't.

When Babes catches me looking, she mutters, "What you staring at? You get eye problems?"

"No," I tell her. So much for snappy comebacks.

"Team yell," Rudy starts. "T-E-A-M, yea team!" He winks at me.

"I keep telling myself, they just mad, going pass," Sterling says.

"You wish," I tell him.

The night gets colder. From the corner of my eye, I see Von walking toward the bathroom between games. I get up and follow her. I don't know what makes me do things like this. But every time I see Von, I feel weak inside. I know that's love. Grandma always says, "Never be afraid to love another girl."

I'm right behind her. "Von?" I say softly. "Von, you real mad at me?" Stupid question, I know.

"What you think, hah, Louie?" She's ready to walk out of the bathroom, but I grab her arm. She yanks herself away. "How come, Louie? Why you squealed on me?"

Von makes me so mad, but I don't cry. "Then why you let Babes kick my ass, Von, hah?" I ask. "You were right there. I seen you sitting on the toilet."

"That was your fault. See, that's the bottom line right there, Louie. You never did accept Babes." Von's so mad, her eyes begin to tear. "You never did accept *me*. How you like that, Louie?"

I should stop myself and tell her sorry and make Von feel better, but I continue blaming her. "And where you was, Von, when my mother came home? I called you and you make Babes more important than me? And you know how messed up I get when my mother come around, right, Von? I always be your number one. Yeah, right."

"Why do I make Babes more important than you? Think, Louie. She IS more important than you."

"Liar. You the liar."

"You don't get it, yeah, Louie? Maybe you the one half-stupid, hah, what you think?"

"You the half-stupid Portagee," I sneer. "I felt like a nothing piece of shit when we was all in the hotel room. You think you the only one who get hard life, Von, but get other people hurting, too. I lied to my grandma for so long. But you so selfish, you only think about you. And that's why you so stupid."

Von comes right up to my face. "You stupid," she whispers. "And you shut your mouth, you hear me, you little nobody? You are *nothing* to me. You keep your big mouth shut before I have to bust you up myself." Von walks out into the big, bright lights of the field; she knows I'm watching, and she spits on the grass.

47.

One of the Boys

Grandma picks me up from school. Von doesn't ride home with us anymore. She rides home with Babes. I watch Von walk up to Babes's truck in the high school parking lot. Babes takes her backpack and puts it in the truck. They sit in the cab and share a cigarette. I watch Von's easy laughter and Babes's animated expressions. Von offers Babes a sip of her soda. They talk and laugh until Kyle arrives. Sometimes Von turns and looks around, as if she senses me looking at her.

"Emi-lou," Grandma calls to me from her car, "c'mon, get in and shake a leg. Stop daydreaming. Plenny cars behind me, you know." Ever since the blow-up with the Vierras, Grandma's really been hard on me.

"You only fourteen, gunfunnit you, Emi-lou," she says all the time. "That's when your mother started—no, before that, maybe eleven. But thirteen, she was full-blown—sleeping around, gum-snapping, lip gloss, boobs hanging out, hickeys on her neck—know what I mean? Sneaking around and lying all the time. I felt so sorry for your grandpa. Nothing we did could make her stop. I messed up with all my daughters," she says pausing. "So I know I have to make things right with you."

I guess that's why every time Sterling and I make plans, she interrogates me or chaperones us. In a lot of ways, I don't mind and neither does Sterling. We do a lot of things with my grandma. But I can tell she's become suspicious of me.

Grandma pulls slowly into our driveway. Aunty Vicky's on the phone. I snub her and go straight to my room. She takes the phone into her bedroom. "Emi-lou," Grandma calls from the living room. "Sterling's here."

He talks with grandma for a while and when she steps onto the lanai to water her orchids, we sit together on the sofa to talk. He lights a cigarette. "Mrs. Kaya, I can smoke inside?"

"Um," she says, waving him off to tend to her plants.

"I gotta stop this," he says. "Ain't helping my game."

"Then stop," I tell him.

"I only do this to make big-man, nobody can stop me, but it ain't me. Aw hell, I hate drinking and smoking dope, too. Feeling all bobo and high," he admits.

"Why you have to make big-man?" I ask him.

"I don't know. Everybody, all the boys going one way, everybody thinking the same, doing the same thing. I no like stand out from the crowd. I like blend. You don't know what it's like being one of the boiz. Hard to be different."

"Like Von," I tell him.

"She get guts, man," he says.

"Like being with me."

Sterling says nothing for a long time. He stares out toward the street. Little kids play with a water hose; next door, my neighbor waters his anthuriums. "Von been calling me up," he says skirting the subject. "Asking me about my mother, small stuff. We talk almost every day."

"Every day? You talk about me?" I ask. Sterling doesn't answer.

"She asks about you," he says. "She just getting it all off her chest."

"So she talking stink behind my back?"

"That's what you really think? Get a grip." After a long silence, Sterling continues. "She telling me all the crap everybody talking."

"About what?" I ask.

"Some about you. Most about me. They talking about me, Louie."

I don't want to hear this. It's leading up to getting rid of the fat chick with no friends. I see myself being erased from the picture. "I miss Von," I tell him.

"What, Louie?"

"She never looks at me, nothing. That's why I'm nobody."

He puts his warm hands on my face and winds his legs with mine. I feel a wave of something strong wash over my whole body. Lips soft on my neck, hands slide over me, easy and slow.

"Emi-lou?" Grandma calls, "Sterling? You ready to play?"

"Golf," he whispers.

"Yeah, golf."

48.
Threes

Bad luck coming in threes is the worst of all the Japanese superstitions. Don't sleep with your feet to the door, don't clip your toenails at night, don't whistle in the dark—I did all of that and nothing ever happened to me. But this bad luck coming in threes thing, there's always three bad things that happen. Always.

One:

I don't know who's spreading rumors about me, but there's plenty going around. I was a lez with Von, and Babes broke us up. I'm a bi, but turned back to lez because I threw myself at Sterling, who didn't like me back. I hate Yvonne Vierra and said I can take her on any day. I hate Babes Hinano and want a rematch at the A-building bathroom. I love Kyle Kiyabu. I hate Genevieve Ching. I secretly love Genevieve Ching. I'm a fat hag hanging around with Rudy Rudman. Well, that one's the closest to the truth.

"Honey-chile," Rudy whispers to me in the library,

"if there was a *National Enquirer*, Hilo version, you be the cover girl every week."

Two:

I've been gaining back some of my weight. My clothes feel snug and my grandma's been on my case about it. I can't tell her that the reason I'm gaining back my weight is because my diet pill, laxative, and diuretic shoplifter of a personal trainer is no longer my friend for life. That and food makes me feel warm inside. I get more and more numb with every bite I take. Food makes me forget.

"No worry," Rudy tells me. "You ain't Emi-fat. Not yet. Ho, let me tell you girl, I remember Emi-fat. She made the earth move under my feet," he sings.

"But I getting there," I tell him.

"Yeah, you better stop pigging out, Petunia, 'cause right now, you Chunky-lou. Next month, you be back to rash between the thighs, pass me my vitamin E cream, please, thank you very much. What your man said about the flab?"

"Nothing," I tell him. "But he been acting strange like he get stuff on his mind that he not telling."

"Um-hum, girl, you heading for the fall, the back door, the see ya, the laters alligators, the–"

"I get it."

"And see your hairdresser, girl. Your dark roots is atrocious."

And three:

Babes Hinano is really not through with me. After newswriting class, Babes sometimes waits for Kyle. She gives me a smug eyebrow jerk if I'm walking out with

Sterling. But for the past few days, he's been out with the flu.

I stay after the bell rings to avoid her. But on this day, Babes comes into the room. "Eh," she tells me. "You like know the best thing I heard?"

I look up from my work. "What?"

"Your *friend*, Sterling Jardine, went to the athletic banquet at the Hilo Hawaiian Hotel with none other than Viva Ching."

"Not, you lie. He said he wasn't going."

Babes laughs when she realizes that I really haven't heard. "All the boys went and we was right there." Babes sits down on the far side of the room. "Yes, you heard it, Louie, you big loser–Genevieve. Oh, this is rich, man. 'Oh, only friends-kine.' That's what your *friend* telling everybody."

Babes walks up to my desk and puts her hands on my papers. "And here comes the best part. You know that night after the homecoming rally was pau, Sterling and Viva in his truck, yes, this is the best–they did it. That's what Viva herself told me."

I cannot move, my body, my mouth, nothing. "For the boys you gotta look right and be seen with the right chicks, and you, Louie, you just ain't right."

I'm so good at keeping it all inside, but I feel it all coming up to my throat, my face, my breathing uneven. I put my head on my desk. When I turn toward the door, I see Von urging Babes to leave the room, to leave me alone.

49.
A Gold Band on Her Left Finger

When my hand picks up the phone, my head's wondering who I'm going to call. My heart already knows it. I dial Von's phone number. I should've planned how I was going to say it or what I was going to ask. I should've known better than to start busting it all out on Von. Who did I think I was? I'm the big squealer, the liar, the little nothing to nobody.

"Hello? Who this? Hello? Hello? Hey, who's this, man, speak up."

"I–"

"What? Who's this? Hello?"

"Vo . . . "

"Babes? Hello?"

I hang up the line.

I think about Von sitting on the tin roof of her house and pouring beer in my hair and licking my face, full of beer, and laughing with Von, massaging lemon juice and beer into my long hair. That's what I remember.

I don't know if Von knows it was me who called her,

but the next night is poker night, and Von comes. I can't believe it when she comes through our back door. It's actually Von.

Aunty Vicky plays the sixth hand sometimes if Uncle Ken doesn't come. She's getting out the mochi crunch and setting up the poker chips. "Eh, Von," she says, "long time no smell, man." And when I come out of the kitchen, I see her in my house. My stomach feels light, like when the phone rings and I'm hoping that it's Sterling.

"Eh, Louie," she tells me. I'm feeling all funny inside but my grandma breaks in and she hugs Von real tight.

"Ho, Aunty Lea," she complains, "you going bust my gut." Then Grandma kisses Von on the head.

"I miss you, Yvonne Shigeko," Grandma says, holding Von in a longer than normal embrace.

"No call me that," Von complains as she smiles with Grandma.

Uncle Charlie starts grumbling about his insurance and how it doesn't cover all the visits Von had to the shrink, so he says he told the guy, "Eh, brah, you not even helping my kid. Even I could do better job than you. Me and my wife, I tell you, gunfunnit." And that was the last time Von had to go to the psychologist. "Never even cure her. I mean, help her *understand* herself."

"Charlie, my dear, you're getting there, honey, you're getting there. Sometimes his words are harsh, but his heart is finally back in his body." Aunty Etsuko's so patient with everybody, especially Uncle Charlie.

Before Uncle can rant and rave about his next problem, the high price of gas in Hawaii, or his high cholesterol and receding hairline, I wipe my hands on the dish towel and head-jerk Von to follow me. She comes easily. We go outside by the garage. I light a mosquito punk and clip it with a clothespin to an old tuna can.

We're kind of stiff at first. Von's wearing a gold band on her left ring finger. She's looking up at the clouds in the black sky. Then all of a sudden, she tells me, "So how come you called me the other night?"

"How you knew was me, Von?" I ask her. I'm so amazed. I'm thinking we're really connected as one after all, blood to blood, V-a-L, and she really can read my mind.

"I knew was you 'cause I called everybody else that usually call me, and they said they never called me, so I figure, had to be you. Whassup?"

Thoughts run through my head. I want Von to tell me things about herself first. Who gave her the ring? What about Babes? Has she spoken to Sterling about me? Or Viva?

"I don't know where Sterling and me stay right now," I blurt out. Von nods. "Why he doing this to me? You think he like Viva?" I want Von to tell me what she knows, if she even wants to tell me. But this thing about Sterling and Viva has been really killing me. "I mean, well, Babes shoved it in my face about the athletic banquet. You went?"

Von nods slowly. "Me, Kyle, and Babes went stag. And Sterling was with–"

I want to die. "Why? 'Cause I getting fat? You think I should tint my hair like Viva again?" Von twirls her ring. "Tell me, please."

Von looks me straight in the eye. "He ain't Mister Perfect, Louie. I tell you, I his friend, but if you and me was—"

"Was what?" I ask. "Friends?"

"If we was, I still think wouldn't be my place to tell you. Get some things you best be figuring out yourself." Von looks away from me.

"Please, tell me," I beg. Something seethes between Von and me, an unsettled churning. "Just tell me."

"He never did fully make up his mind," Von says. "He knows he really like you, but he know the boiz would approve of Viva. You know, for his rep. And he just ain't into one, you know, commitment."

"Somebody dunk my head in a vat of boiling oil, please, put me out of my misery." I stare blankly at the shifting moon, the haze of dark clouds.

"Until he figures out what he like," Von says to me, "no let him dangle you on one string." She puts her hand on my knee and squeezes it tight.

I realize how much I've missed her. It's quiet for a long time. I listen to the laughter of the adults inside. "How come we ain't talking about me and you, Von?" I ask her at last. "I mean, what happen to us?" She doesn't talk for a long time. She continues to play with the gold band on her finger.

"Louie," she says. "I no get you, man. I mean, this all about you. You like know something? I still all bust up 'cause of what you told your grandma about me and Babes. I mean, I know was Vicky who squealed, but still, you told. Yeah, was wrong for me to do all that in the same room with you. That was uncool, but—"

"It was uncool. You ain't perfect, either, Von." She grimaces. "But I sorry."

"Sorry ain't going do, you know what I mean? I gotta tell you, Louie, that what I am, I am. My mother slowly helping my father get a grip. I don't know—that's just the way it is. And what gets me, is that you the best thing I ever had, you my blood, and you the one broke me apart. I like you know, Louie, it wasn't easy to talk to you about this. And after that day at the beach, I thought you was with me, man, all the way. I pretty messed up, so your sorry to me means—"

"Too many sorries, Von."

"Yeah, Louie, too many sorries." She looks away at the street. She looks at her watch and then puts her face in both hands.

"She my friend first, Louie," she says, "a good friend, like you, but not like you. I mean, more than me and you. Babes and me, we—"

"Von," I tell her. "Eh, Von. This is deep, man, deeper than the deep blue sea." She looks up slowly—smiling crookedly and small. Then we laugh just a little bit, Von and me.

50.
Somebody Good to Me

Von sleeps over at my house that night. In the morning, I wake up early and put the blanket nicely over her curled body. Grandma's in the kitchen and she helps me make the biggest Portuguese sausage, eggs, rice, Japanese popcorn tea, and waffles from scratch, a big breakfast for Von.

And it doesn't change things much, the way things used to be—but my grandma helps me to understand that nothing can ever be how it used to be. "Life ain't that way," she tells me. "You always move on to what's next. So Yvonne don't call three times a day like she use to, she came poker night already and slept over. That's a start. You have to think that way."

"And me, too," I tell her. "I gotta move on, too."

"What you talking about?" she asks as the steam from the hot rice rises from the pot.

"I ain't being a stinker to Rudy no more. And tell you the truth, I like student gov. Why should I feel shame? Maybe I join one club with him."

"Yeah, you keep moving on, too, Emi-lou," my grandma says. "And Von—she told me she like ride home with us from school. Pretty soon, she be catching ride with us in the morning, but you take things one moment at a time."

Grandma put it to me like this: "Could you trust your mother with all your heart after all the times she let you down? See what I mean? Could you ever trust her?"

Of course, the answer is no. Each time, the hurt feels less sore until you feel nothing for that person so that your body and heart don't need to feel like they're burning and pulling apart.

"Well, that's the same with Yvonne. You have to give her time and make her know that you understand and you ain't ever going judge her again. Emi-lou, you know she cannot change, right? You cannot force somebody to be who you want them to be."

"Yeah, but she cannot do that to me, too."

"And she shouldn't." I turn to watch Von's sleeping body rustle under the blanket.

"It's okay, right, Grandma, when girls love girls? I mean, really love each other."

My grandma is silent for a long time. "Of course it is. Love is complicated and way more than just sex. But you take a little time with all this, your whole life if you have to." My grandma laughs, but I think she really means it. "Yvonne," my grandma says, "is still somebody good to me."

Good is Von combing my hair.

Good is the sound of Von sleeping on the floor futon in my bedroom.

Good is summer and night ball games, green neon field at Carvalho Park.

Good is swimming at Four Miles.

Good is Von and I talking story.

Good is a name. My name.

Not Jerry Rapoza's name.

Not Roxanne Kaye's altered name.

My name.

Name me: Emi-lou Kaya.

51.
Wanting to Be

She doesn't call me every day. But I feel this peace inside. That's something to hang on to after I finish taking a bath and the wind's cutting through my bedroom window, and I sleep a little bit easier.

I want to figure out what I can do to make things go smooth. What can I do to make Von know that I'm not a nobody–that I'm something to her and her to me.

Two weeks into summer, Aunty Vicky's putting on her baseball pants and long-sleeved T-shirt under her old Hilo Astros shirt. There's holes from all the other seasons she played. She gets her shoes and starts to brush them with an old coconut brush.

"So what, Louie? Like warm bench again, or you get too much pride? Sheez, you such a scrub. Do me a favor and stay away from league this year. I had hard time hold my head up last season with you so junk and all."

"Why?" I tell her. "Only our team knew I was junk. I hardly played. But I got kind of better by the end of the season. Anyway, I taking clarinet lessons, algebra, and typing this summer with Rudy."

"Oh, yes, you did play enough to embarrass me," she says.

"What?"

"Aunty Erma put you in right field when us played Pāhala and we was up fifteen to three."

"Oh, wow, one minute in right field."

"Yeah, one minute and one missed pop fly from Carly Espinoza."

Aunty Vicky's got a good memory for bad memories.

"No wise off, Louie. Just do me a favor and stay home bake peanut butter cookies with Rudy Rudman. 'Cause I don't think none of the girls like you around."

I look at my aunty Vicky's face and I swear, the light on her face is not like anything I've ever seen before. It's a revealing yellow light. And the words "I don't think none of the girls" repeat in my head.

No, one of the girls might want me there. And *I* want to be there. There to get better at softball, there to be a player not a quitter, there to stop choking, there to show Coach Kaaina that I can take it, there because I can support a friend's dream for a scholarship, there because I *want* to be there.

"Aunty Vicky, wait. I am playing this summer. Even if only two minutes this season. It ain't about that. It's about wanting it for me."

"Hah? What you talking about? Stay home."

"Wait for me." I run to my room and grab my baseball pants and a tank top. I dig in the closet for the glove Uncle Charlie gave me. And I search for Von's old cleats that she gave me when Uncle bought her new softball shoes in the middle of last season.

"Please, Aunty Vicky, please take me." I'm just about ready to do anything for her to give me a ride to Carvalho Park.

"No way, Emi-lou. You ain't going be seen with me. Nobody like you turn out, especially Aunty Erma. Stay home." She grabs her keys and head out the door.

"I know I junk," I tell her, "but I can get better."

"Oh, please, you below junk."

I get my bike from behind the garage and pump the tires fast. I ride up to the park with my glove tucked under my arm. I know what I have to do.

52.
Somebody

Coach Kaaina sees me first. She crushes her paper cup and shakes her head. "Take a lap," she yells at me before I even have a chance to do anything wrong at practice.

Choochie and Rae five me low. Anita sits in the stands with Rudy who waves at me. Von's in the outfield warming up with Herline Santos. She doesn't see me coming. When she finally sees me she yells, "What you doing here, Louie-Louie? You going get punish this season, I tell you." She throws the softball at me. I catch it firmly with my bare hand. "Nice reflex," she says.

"Where Von go—"

And Von finishes with little enthusiasm, "Louie-Louie go. Finish your lap and come back warm-up with Herline and me."

"I here to *play* this season, Von." I stop and run in place so Coach Kaaina won't get mad at me. Then I throw the softball back at Von.

"Nice arm, good follow-through," she says, nodding.

"I like play this time for me. Nothing else, know what I mean, Von?"

"If I thinking what you mean, then yeah, I help you this season. You here to play, not watch over me, right, Louie?"

"Or judge you."

"Okay, then, I know what you mean." Von looks down and digs her shoes into the grass. "You be the sub for the sub right fielder, maybe fifteenth batter, but so what? You here to play."

"C'mon, c'mon. Sheez, lovers' reunion?" Herline yells at Von. I don't care. They can all say what they want, spread all the rumors they like. I don't care. Babes jogs over.

"How you like Von's ring, Louie?" Babes asks. I know she's testing me, eyeing me up and down, and snapping a softball in her glove.

"It's a nice ring. I saw it the other night," I whisper. "I happy for you."

I run the rest of my lap. I don't even look back to see what Babes thought of what I said, because I'm not lying. I mean it. I'm happy if Von's happy.

I run up to the dugout and see Viva leaning on the fence in a tight bodysuit and jeans shorts. She's got her long, ehu-tinted hair in a ponytail coming out the back side of her baseball cap.

She's talking to Sterling. My first impulse is to run away, to find Von, to go home.

"Get lost," Viva tells me.

"Louie," Sterling says, "wait, wait for me." He gets up off the bench.

222

"Sterling," Viva calls. "Where you going?" The girls all turn to watch. He puts his hand on my shoulder to stop me and then takes my hand in his.

"Show's over," Von yells at the girls.

"Listen to me," Sterling says, "I was going call you after practice. What you doing here? You going play again? You sure?"

"Determined," I answer.

"Aunty Erma," Viva yells, "you going let Emi-lou play this summer? Send her home. I cannot believe this. I thought Crimson was playing. Sterling, you come back here."

Sterling walks with me toward the first base bleachers. We sit down and say nothing for a little while. "I helping my grandma coach," he tells me softly.

"Big deal," I tell him.

"I barely finish my sophomore year."

"So? Big deal two times," I repeat.

"I don't know if I can play volleyball 'cause my grade point was down real low."

"Good for you. You deserve it for being a liar." I give him a dirty stink eye.

Sterling pauses and makes his leg touch mine. "I have to go summer school to raise my GPA."

"I going summer school to take algebra," I tell him in an I-could-care-less monotone.

"Good, we go together. I mean summer school."

"Dream on," I tell him. "Go with your girl, Viva."

Sterling looks toward the river by the gym. "I messed up big time, Louie. I went nuts little bit and what I did to you, I–"

"Yep," I tell him, "you went nuts and then you went to the athletic banquet with Genevieve Ching. Then you got demoted from Mr. Perfect to Mr. Imperfect full of flaws and no backbone, which you had been all along but I was too stupid to see."

"Huh?"

I put my glove on my lap. "You heard me."

"Louie, you have to know, I been thinking hard—you have to know that from the time at Hāpuna Beach," he says slowly.

"What? You pitied the white whale?"

"No," he says moving closer to me, "was something about the way you was just like me, so lost and so—"

"Fat?"

"C'mon, no and yes. I don't know. I keep telling Baron and Levi that some girls, they nice to look at and all that—but hell, was easier if I told them I was baby-sitting."

"Jerk."

"And Louie, you ain't shame of your brains. I mean, that's good and bad. You smart and that ain't typical. I don't know. The guys no like that kine girls."

"Well, thanks for the talk, Sterling. Friend." I get up to leave, but he takes my hand in his.

I pull my hand away.

"I mean, I did go to the stupid banquet with Viva like some stupid trophy date, I mean, she wore the same red gown. Was bad. But I like you know, Louie, and it's my word against hers, I never did nothing with her."

"So you say. Big deal," I tell him at last, "you took her, the end."

"Ask Von what she told me when I called her the next day?"

"Why should I? I don't care."

"I had to see for sure what I really wanted," he says.

"And now you know *for sure*?" I ask him sarcastically.

"Yes."

"Yeah, right. What Von said?"

"As her ex-shrink would say, I insecure with low self-esteem and too worried about peer pressure–" Sterling touches my hair. "She said that you deserve the truth. We all do. We all been jerks to each other, but I was the biggest." He tilts his head back and forth as he looks me over. "I like your hair black like this," he says. "No need tint no more."

"No tell me what to do," I say. "No tell me all your thoughts and feelings. Just no tell me nothing. And while you at it–" I stop. And then, I start nodding.

"What?"

"You right," I say slowly. I don't tell Sterling just yet, but the truth is that I realize that I've been a pretty big jerk myself.

"Huh?" he asks.

"About the black hair."

I look out toward where Von's warming up with Babes and Herline. I watch her long body and smooth movement. I breathe deeply.

Yvonne Shigeko Vierra.

She sees us looking at her and comes running over. "So what, Sterling? When you watching spooky movies at Louie's house with her Grandma? I like come."

Sterling looks at me, then at his strong brown hands. "We starting over. We taking this from when I gave Louie the maunaloa lei at last year's softball awards. No, back to that day at Hāpuna Beach–"

Von leans on the fence. Babes walks over and stands next to her. They look at each other that way, the way that hurt me before, the way that Von will never look at me but makes her shine from the inside out.

"So what you think, Louie?" Sterling asks. "Good place to go from, or what?"

"Maybe."

"Friends. Deep in *like*," he says.

"I don't know if I even like you at this point," I tell him.

Von comes around the fence and sits on the bleachers next to Sterling.

"We start from who going to teach Louie how to catch one fly ball and throw to first base. Batting, teach her batting. Louie," Von says, "we got nowhere to go but up. All of us."

"I'm there for losing a few pounds with Louie," Babes says. "But only if Von the trainer again." She looks at the three of us, smiles briefly, then runs back onto the field. "And spooky movies. Count me in."

"And I ain't hiding nobody anymore, especially 'cause you somebody to me," Sterling says. He puts his arm around my waist and his other arm around Von. I know the smell of his clothes.

"Louie," Von says, "he right. We start over. No more disrespect."

Sterling kisses Von on her forehead then puts his

face in my hair, and takes a deep breath. "I missed you," he whispers.

"This is deep," Von starts.

"Deeper than the deep blue sea," I finish.

The lights go on over the field. I listen to the hum of the breakers, the orange-white light buzzing of green on the field at Carvalho Park. Stay in the moment, like Grandma says, this moment of beginning, this moment of Sterling, Von, and me in the familiar lights of Carvalho Park.

My deepest thanks to the following people:

To Mel, for storytelling and friendship for this lifetime, blessing upon blessing. Mimi and Deedee, Lani-girl and Makamae. Shari at Magic Island, for it's so busy, busy, busy reminders, take a bath, you'll feel better. Nancy, for your life that keeps coming up in books, Claire, for utter bravery, Donna, for years that never pass, and Don, for the Ramona the Pest from that bookstore on Columbus.

To Donna Bray for brilliant guidance and resurrection of the work.

To Susan Bergholz for sage advice and being with me always. No more yeahyeahyeahs from these lips! Ito, love.

To Josie Woll, Dora Jean Ota, Liz Watanabe, Marsha Akamu, Grandma Maria, Grandpa Camilo, Naomi Grossman, and Crisana Cook, for healing and hearing so clearly, the words and feelings in the jargon.

To Mari Ann Arveson, Janice Simon, Aunty Clara Kawasaki, Kristi Lucas, Joy Sakai, and Kristi Lane, who listened to him sing.

To Booth Pool near the beautiful la'amia tree, Joanne, Amy, Tad, Genell, Tomi, Ryan, Kamaile.

To Nohea Kanaka'ole, Aunty Bridget, Aunty Pali, Aunty Katherine, Ellen, Heidi, Marlene Inter, Mrs. White, LuAnn Ocalada, and Denise Webb who teach.

To Melinda Schram, Holly Stepanuik, and Keith Helelā from the mommy on P-10, the world on P-2.

To Morgan Blair, light walking.

To Cora Yee for Yin & Yang, sista artist wife.

To my friends at Bamboo Ridge Press, in spite of dysfunction, marketing, publicity, fundraising, benefit nights, and general grouchiness, because you my family; special thanks to Nora Okja Keller, never an island in a whirlwind.

To Doreen and Robert Teixeira, Tom and Trudi Cannon, Cori, Travis, and BK, for the best of times in the town house.

To Dr. Mike and Dr. Lee at DATA 1 in Honolulu, no matter how much I bothered you, Gerald and Steve for minimal complaints and a kick in my technological ass to the twenty-first century, not.

To another Emi (Sumida) from Ann Arbor, Michigan, thank you for the wonderful name and always remember Gail said you will be a teenager till forty-one.

To Jean and Harry, for a liberal, open-minded house. Mona with grandchild number three, Kathy of the Charlie-mommy, and Carla bring home the bucks, baby.

To Charlene Nobriga, Sista, without you there is no us, strength and wellness, the angels on your shoulders always.

To John TSYI, for your fighting spirit that is well and whole, believe it and know it.

To John, the best play-by-play broadcaster of volleyball and softball games that happened in my writing room with sky light and trains.

229